Second Coming
or Second Trade-off:
Contemporary & Relevant
Literature during the Pandemic

Otis D. Alexander

Acknowledgement

Sincere thanks and appreciations to the writers for participating in this worthwhile project of thoughts and feelings. They allowed the community to lean on their shoulders.

Beryl Agnes Watson Shaw of Frederiksted, Virgin Islands and Helen D. Laurence of West Palm Beach, Florida are given thanks and appreciations for taking the time to read this work.

Without the Florida Memorial University Library and the Little River Branch of the Miami Regional Public Library, this activity would not have been completed. Special thanks to Cheryl Wilcher, Director at Florida memorial University and Tristan Miller, Branch Manager at Little River for their understanding and support.

The following writers are greatly appreciated for the original work; their time and energy; and their humanity. They are working through difficult times where they are in the middle of a devastating pandemic and the protests of racial injustice. Therefore, "hats off" to Blair E. Alexander Sr., Brandon Trent Alexander, Ayana Askew, Vanessa Araujo, Askhat Aubakirov, Freddie Barnes, Felicia A. Andrews Bryant, Neal "Panta X" Carrington, Muriel "Myrrh" Cauthen, Hamza Chafki, Janet Darby, Janell Davis, John Riley Dungee, I, Nabil Eddoumi, Cynthia Rochelle Clarambeau Hall, William Ashanti Hobbs III, James Arthur Holmes, Pamela Browne Jafari, Argarita Johnson-Palavicini, Keith Randall Knatt, II, Barry Koplen, Helen D. Laurence, Frances M. Laveau, André Licencier, Winifred "Oyoko" Loving, Linda Jones Malonson,

Second Coming or Second Trade-off: Contemporary & Relevant Literature during the Pandemic

Otis D. Alexander

ISBN: 978-1-63652-026-1

Beyond The Book Case
New York,   London,   Accra

Available wherever books are sold.
Online at: MANSABOOKS.COM

Michael Darnell Marks II, Julius E. McCullough, Yuri Millien, Fred Motley, Georgette Norman, Shirley White Smith Nottingham, Diane Wilson Onwuchekwa, Erick Payan, Arthur Petersen, Cipriani A. Phillip Jr., Alvin Pondexter, Julian Rolle, Beryl A. Watson Shaw, Rose Mary Stiffin, Jeffrey Dean Swain, Onika M. Thomas, Avicia B. Hooper Thorpe, Dinizulu Gene Tinne, André M. Titus Jr., Lovel Toran Waiters, Thomas Walker II, Ronald Rodney White, AcNeal L. Williams, Catherine I. Williams, and David Zuber. They are greatly appreciated for usage permission of their writings. Their global outlook is welcome.

The poetry of Nancy Cunard, Paul Laurence Dunbar, Jessie Redmon Fauset, Georgia Douglas Johnson, Claude McKay, and William Butler Yeats are materials that are in public domain or fair usage. Therefore, libations have been poured on "Mother Earth" for their contributions to the vast body of knowledge. They will forever be celebrated!

The compiler is especially appreciative to Dr. Adele D. Allen for extending permission for the inclusion of the poetry of her grandaunt, Mrs. Avicia B. Hooper Thorpe. Permission to use the work of John Riley Dungee, I has been extended by granddaughter, Adrienne Dungee Felton. Prof. Jakelin Miranda is appreciated for connected me to the writers of Miami's Cuban community. Mark S. Askew, Sr. is recognized for assisting me with pictures and accurate information regarding biographical sketches. Vertez Burks passed on the poetry of the late Lovel Toran Waiters. Burks is appreciated for her thoughtfulness.

Dedication

To the memory of those who transitioned during the pandemic as well as:

Abdirahman Abdi
Ahmaud Arbery
Chris Beaty
Sandra Bland
Emantic Fitzgerald Bradford Jr.
Brandon Brocious
Rayshard Brooks
Eric Brown
Michael Brown
D'Andre Campbell
Victor Cazares Jr.
David Dorn
George Floyd
Robert Forbes
Marvin François
Abdi Gani
James Garcia
Jorge Gomez
Jose Gutierrez
Javar Harrell
Anna Hiavka
Mahamud Hirsi
Calvin Horton Jr.
Botham Jean
Rueben Johnson
Italia Kelly

Second Coming

David Josiah Lawson
Hakeem Littleton
Andrew Loku
Charleena Lyles
Dorian Murrell
Regis Korchinski-Paquet
Trayvon Martin
David McAtee
Elijah McClain
Tony McDade
Ann O'keefe
Barry Perkins III
Marcus-David Peters
Nina Pop
James Scurlock
Daniel Shaver
Rubin Stacey
Breonna Taylor
John Tiggs
Emmett Till
Marquis Tousant
Samwel Uko
Patrick Underwood
Francis Ricardo "Ricky" West

Contents

8

Second Coming

9

INTRODUCTION

A "Magic Moment" that has turned the world upside down stimulated the project. It is intended to allow expression based on the relevant situation- mental, physical, political, social, and economic- that we are encountering with "COVID19," "Black Lives Matter," and the "global revelation" that is being witnessed now to dismantle structural racism/classicism. Moreover, the title of this work, Second Coming is based on the poem of William Butler Yeats, "The Second Coming," that led Chinua Achebe to write the award-winning book, *Things Fall Apart*.

With the nouveaux coronavirus and how it has affected the entire globe, livelihoods, lifestyles, and human existence have been interrupted. This is a pandemic and an epidemic that challenges hope for many. Of course, this is not the first time nor the last that a communicable disease will come into our space and divide our thoughts as well as force us to pool our humanity.

In March 2020, the nouveaux coronavirus took over the world creating chaos in the minds of all humans, panic, and uncertainty about public health. It became frightening when the health experts predicted that not only are we at risk now but also a heavy second wave of infections will be expected. This virus is bad! Is this the "second coming" that William Butler Yeats wrote about in 1919, after the end of World War I? I did not have any plans of reading about Yeats after completing an undergraduate course in literature.

Democratic and Republican senators urged the White House to prepare for a double dose of Covid-19 and flu outbreaks in the fall. Yes, it is bad and the cases continue rise in the millions.

During World War I, the government debt recently plunged to record lows, as financial institutions poured funds into comfortable assets to ensure that a sizable amount of money would be set aside for the wartime economy. However, this time, it has been proven that even more funding should be allocated for the anticipated for pandemics and healthcare.

As the coronavirus pandemic continues to penetrate globally, remain physically distanced but get as close as possible through the power of the imagination. Here, you will see the reflective active and reflective passive aspects of literature at its best. They include wonderful ideas and concepts regarding global perspectives. These ideas and concepts form the essence of this publication. In addition, all of the contributors in this work are far from being in an envelope or vacuum. They have an accurate understanding of relevant cultural and historical characteristics. In other words, they know the streets, the "hallowed halls," and approach life as it is. They are problem solvers working through literature.

Therefore, all of the writers and researchers have come together to do their part in soothing the pain, sharing their thoughts, and making the world comfortable for the moment because it is in the now and William Butler Yeats kept the secret with his old but always current poem- "The Second

Coming!" In addition, Achebe knew that something would fall apart as the world celebrates the ending of a brutal 400 years of historical encounters. Are we still anticipating something that will soon occur? What is the trade-off?

Otis D. Alexander

FROM THE SOUL

"The Racial Equality Bugaboo" by John Riley Dungee, I

They're raising a horrible hullabaloo
About the racial equality bugaboo.
They're rummaging ancestral trees
And probing into pedigrees,
Examining analogies,
Comparing genealogies,
Dissecting one another's veins,
Detecting microscopic strains
To demonstrate authority
For race superiority.

'Tis arbitrarily decreed
That only that peculiar breed,
Whose ichor is distinctly blue,
And strictly Nordic thru and thru,
With stipulations can comply,
And critically qualify.
Discrimination, agitation,
Separation, legislation,
Clamor for effectuation
Of the stern determination
That this Nordic purity
Remain in perpetuity.

Now this grandiloquent design
Is theoretically fine,
But in its actualities
Is punctured full of fallacies.
For who can certainly declare

Just who these nifty Nordics are?
All selections of connections,
Manifold amalgamations,
And untold adulterations
Constitute a complication
That defies elucidation,
And confirms the declaration
That no mortal can declare
Who the haughty Nordics are.

And furthermore, I must relate
That this conglomerated state
Is but the natural fruition
Of the Nordics' own volition.
Upon their own initiation
They contrived the situation
That produced amalgamation,
And obliterates the traces
That identify the races.
Hence their fanciful seclusion
Is a farcical delusion
That denies unwilling eyes'
Ability to realize
That they are coming to their own,
And reaping simply what they've sown.
However, since they now intend
By all inventions to amend
The circumstances that offend,
It seems to me the proper course
Would staunch the streamlet at its source.
Consistency would reprobate
Relations that originate
Conditions they would obviate.
Instead, they stultify their cause
With their inconsequential laws,
Whose impotent verbosity

Breathes only animosity,
And stupidly defeats the ends
Its phraseology intends.

Exclusively they designate
For most incorrigible hate
All evidencing any fraction
Or trace of African extraction.
They vent their sworn determination
To damn us with humiliation,
Indignity and degradation.
They specify where we shall eat,
And where we are to take a seat.
They designate where we may ride,
Likewise, where we may reside.
They shout vociferous negation
On virtuous association,
While disguised affiliations
And amphibian emanations
Assiduously dissipate
All that they would effectuate.
Instead of these fallacious schemes,
And these impracticable dreams,
I recommend the only plan
That ever could or even can
Assure the Nordic blood salvation
From varicolored infiltration,
And salvage it the residue
Of its inestimable blue,
If Nordic masculinity
Relinquished its affinity
For the captivating graces
Of the varicolored races,
Or could they differentiate
The traces they would isolate,

Second Coming

There'd be no need to advocate,
And no excuse to legislate
Pernicious disabilities
On innocent civilities.

But if this ardent predilection
Defies volitional direction,
Or if the African infection
Eludes censorial detection,
Not all the councils and the courts,
Nor all the arsenals and forts
Can rectify the situation
By statutory regulation.
'Tis vain, therefore, to speculate,
And agitate and legislate,
And senseless, too, is the hullabaloo
About the racial equality bugaboo.

First published in *Random Rhymes:Formal and Dialect Serious and Humorous Racial, Religious, Patriotic and Sentimental* in 1929.
Permission extended   to use in this publication by granddauhter, Adrienne Dungee Felton.

"This Democracy of Ours" by Avicia B. Hooper Thorpe

The white man has carried his prejudice
Wherever he has gone.
In trying to democratize the world, he forgets that
democracy, like charity should begin at home.

Why do we think that our form of government is the best for
all other nations, when everywhere the whites have gone
that have carried their brutality and segregation?

Just think of four hundred million dollars sent abroad to
prevent communism?
When here at home they cannot control their practices of
"Jim Crowism!"

A sheriff putting out a soldier's eyes.
A mob taking the jailer's keys and lynching a Negro,
and saying in court, "yes, I did." Moreover, the judge and
jury saying "Let them go!"

A senator of the United States Congress vituperating his
colored brothers over the air; to retain such a senator at the
colored citizens' expense.
All fair-minded people will agree is unfair.

The poorest of foreigners may enter this country and to the
mayorship of her largest city rise; but the American-born
colored citizen can look forward to no such clear skies.
Just imagine, if you can, in this country and day, a woman
for forty years held a slave!

It is enough to make those early fighters for freedom turn over in their long-forgotten graves.

There are many, many other things that I have not the space to mention; but I hope steps will be taken to remedy them as from time they claim our attention.

How one drop of Negro blood can make a person colored is beyond my power to understand.
Is it determined by mathematical or biological science?
Please answer this question, and one who can.

If we could trace families, it would be interesting to see just how many pure whites there are in this prejudice country.

Then why be so hard on the Negro- at every opportunity showing a slight?
When in so many cases we know not whether a person is colored or white.

It is said that a person does not know who hurt him. I suppose this applies to race relations.
For, just let the whites learn that you have colored blood, and they will certainly change the situation.

In many cases we have been mistakenly accepted for members of the opposite race;
Somehow, they feel that to openly accept us in places for real disgrace.
They will give a job to a German of a Japanese, who, at the first chance, will knife them through and through;

In addition, at the same time say to the Negro, "There is no opening for you."

Oh, yes, we can cook for them; take care of their home, and even help their children to rear.
But for filling a vacancy wherever it occurs- lo the Unwritten law- Colored citizen, you can't work here.

Some even seem to think we crave the right to marry them and they fear amalgamation.
They do not stop to consider that in our race
We have every kind of flower of the Master's creation.

So, it is not intermarriage we seek, but such rights as belongs to the free-
To work, ride, eat, and live where we please,
For these things are a part of liberty,

To be paid for a job according to one's merits rather than the color of skin;
To be allowed to be proud of our race,
Instead of made to feel that to be born black is a sin.

It is said that Ethiopia shall stretch forth her hands. Yes, she shall rise out of her distress.
The Father will not permit one group of His children forever another group oppress.

The Hebrews in Egypt for over four hundred years-
Yes, God's chosen people made slaves,

But in His own good time God delivered them and led their oppressors to
Watery graves.

Why wait for other nations to force your hand, making you to all citizens be just and true?
Form "White America," all other countries
Surely, have their eyes on you!

Said Jesus, "He that sayeth he loves me whom he hath not seen,
And hateth his brother whom he hath seen, is a liar."
If some people get past Saint Peter to behold us in the Heavenly Estate,
I suppose they will leave Heaven to us and depart for the fire.

But even there they will find some of us, and there will be likely be eternal strife.
So, let us live the Golden Rule and work together here, and all enjoy richer, fuller,
More beautiful life.

*Avicia B. Hooper Thorpe wrote this poem in 1947. Permission to include this work has been extended by her niece; Power-of-Attorney, Dr. Adele D. Allen.

Otis D. Alexander
"Exercise in Denial" by Georgette Norman

It was just another
unpainted clapboard house
      dotting the rural southern landscape
    neglected
                ravaged by the elements
              long void of human life

The winter of 1995 would change all that

A friend seeing a white woman jogging along the highway
Decided to ask, "What's the history of that house"
The jogger answered, "That house has no history; It's just a
niggah house"

When told of this exchange
My brain froze
The words reverberated
              "just a niggah house"
           "has no history"
             "a niggah house"
      "no history"

This house
walls in tack
windows still paned though a crack or two
rusted tin roof buckling but covering the frame
           was denied existence
denied its stories
denied its memories

because the "people" dark of skin
who once lived therein
could not be recognized

This house was denied its families
Sunday mornings
holiday cheer
births and deaths
as the design of rocks in the back yard so well establish

denied its kitchen
   beans w/a hock cooking on the stove
               Ba' Bruh's bathing in the wash tub
               Sistah washing clothes in the sink
      and Aunt Lil getting her hair "laid to the side" with the
comb hot from the stove

denied its children playing "Lil Sally Walker" on a clean
swept yard
denied its first new used car parked out front
                     and the pride that comes from actually
getting what you saved two years to get

denied its Chinaberry tree now a stump where
Daddy hung a tire swing one summer day
Bo broke his leg, when he fell trying to build a tree house
the family stood in awe of Uncle Joe's new gray 'n red
   Ford N Series tractor
Daddy carved "G loves E" in a heart after he first saw Mom

Just a niggah house?
No history?

It's amazing the lengths
some will go
to deny
a people
existence

"Judgement in Alabama" by Georgette Norman

Selma
March 8, 1965
mouth stretching in a face deforming yawn
one hand wiping sleep from eyes not yet awake
the other reaching for that 1st cup of coffee
savor its flavor
grab the morning paper

Alabama Police Use Gas and Clubs to Rout Negroes (NYT)
Tear Gas Clubs Halt 600 in Selma March (TWP
Alabama Negro March Explodes Into Bloody Violence with
Police
(Fitchburg Sentinel, Massachusetts)

SCHOCKED from your reverie
you read accounts
which interrupted 'Judgment at Nuremberg'
you missed last night

Outrage over "Bloody Sunday" swept the country
America filled with righteous indignation at the sights and
sounds
of sit-ins
                    traffic blockades
                    demonstrations in solidarity across
the country

Confederacy's guns were not silenced in the Civil War
Racial legacies

of Slavery

Reconstruction

reverberated
and roared loudly
from tear gas throwing
     billy club beating
     horse stomping
     licensed to maim Alabama State Troopers
    and mercenary segregationists
in plain view of photographers and journalist
some so shocked they forgot to document
    helped the fallen
themselves now victims of assault

mayhem escalates in a mix of

             screams from terrified
marchers

fallen beaten bodies on the asphalt

            and cheers from
reveling bystanders

as deputies on horseback swung clubs and rubber tubing
wrapped in barbed wire
     charged ahead
     chasing gasping men,

           women
           children

back
over

the bridge

though they were forced back
they did not fight back.

Edmund Pettus Bridge,
you bear the name
of a white supremacist
But now
You are
a
CIVIL
RIGHTS

"Stain on the Heart of America" by Georgette Norman

Selma
divided racially and geographically
Black/white
Bluff on the west side/Plain on the east
And a river
The Alabama runs through it

On a cold Sunday
   March
   afternoon in 1965
Race, Geography and the Alabama River
  changed the city forever
600 people
   gathered at Brown Chapel AME Church
      silently waked
  except for the sounds of shoes
    wove through West Selma streets
      until they stood at the foot of a
bridge
   stood on the site of the former two-lane swing bridge
       designed for mule
traffic
        hauling
wagonloads of cotton

life blood of the city

symbol of the mind of the white south
  gazed upon its 1940 four-lane replacement

unable to see the other side

Its name, Edmund Pettus

    Lawyer...General in the Confederate

army...Two-time U. S. Senator...Grand

     Dragon of the Alabama realm of the Ku Klux

Klan

   a reminder of

       why

   they

are

  here

The new structure re-newed the structures of white power

Faulker was right, "The Past isn't dead, it's not even Past."

They begin their cross

Montgomery and the Capitol on their mind

Until, they reach the crest

   see the other side of the bridge

  150 armed troopers

         masks

strapped to helmets bearing the Confederate flag,

  hefting billy clubs against open palms,

        mounted on

horses

       and mercenary

segregationists ready for action

  Photographers and journalists poised to document

Undeterred they descend

Two by Two

   they cross

Ordered to turn back...They keep walking
Armed only with the "Call for Justice"
Tear gas explodes
Chaos erupts

Many retreat
      screaming, chased by those entrusted to protect
Others, knocked to the ground
      dragged, brutally assaulted with billy clubs
   and trampled by horses
 lie in bloody crumpled heaps on the asphalt

March 7, 1965, "Bloody Sunday"
A day of infamy unjustified and unjustifiable
Outraged America and the World

The stain of blood shed that day cannot be washed/hosed
away
      too deeply soaked onto the tablet of
American's history

Selma, still racially, geographically and river divided
   but far more than a location
Now a concept
  a mindset
  a reminder that
      must become more than
commemoration
Selma and the Bridge are Sacred Ground...Sacred Space

Walk reverently across the bridge

channel history into action
heed the call

at this intersection on the
Social Justice Road

to make sure all Americans
have equal access to the ballot
walk
walk on
Crossing and re-crossing
Ever vigilant 'til there are no more bridges of injustice to
cross.

Otis D. Alexander

"Oriflamme" by Jessie Redmon Fauset

I think I see her sitting bowed and black,
Stricken and seared with slavery's mortal scars,

Reft of her children, lonely, anguished, yet

Still looking at the stars.

Symbolic mother, we thy myriad sons,

Pounding our stubborn hearts on Freedom's bars,

Clutching our birthright, fight with faces set,

Still visioning the stars!

*This poem is in the public domain.

"Corona ... Evil Adorned" by Frances M. LaVeau

Corona ... Diabolical Crown ... Polished, Embellished, Adorned with

Sparkling Gems, Beautiful Glittering Stones

Cleverly Concealing Impending Shock and Utter Devastation

Infestations ... Horrendous Piercings amid Interlocking Thorns ...

Emboldened by the Evil that Adorned

Cast into the Atmospheric Pressure of Time and of Space ...

Ordained at specific intervals to Burst and Shatter ...

Savagely Dispersing its Poisonous Elements

Splitting Energy, Culling, Deep Cleansing, Silencing Life Forms

Eradicating many ... Mammals and Associates ... Returning them

To the dust from whence they emerged

No signed Contracts set in stone had been given ...

Only the Lies that proceeded from the mouths of Fools

Untruths that Entertained & Nourished Masochistic Members of certain
Societies ...Thieves and Fools ... They who Continually Ingested whatever

Fowl Nonsense they were being Fed

Although there were Signals ... Extremely Powerful
Vibrating the Atmosphere

Even the Deaf could sense and hear them

The Blind Envisioned ... then Witnessed the Light

When the Signal made its Presence known

Then there were Those in Strong Denial ... Continually flipping the Script

As their Idiotic Leader ... labeled it All as Fake News Denial, Using Caustic Retorts , Insults, Harassment

The Narcissistic, Maniacal , Demon Clown at the Helm

Always in a Sadistic Entertainment Mode ... providing his Minions

Zombies and audience of Confused Onlookers

A one-way ticket to his Luxury Villa in the outer
Dimensions of Hades

Air Pollution, Extreme Warmth in November, and Chilly
snowy days in the

Spring ... If April was still considered to be Spring

Global Warming, Fires Raging ... Ice Capped Glaciers
Melting, Rivers

Continually Rising

Greed of Evil Gentry ... Blood Thirsty Killers & Kin

Always Feasting upon the Labors of Disenfranchised
Peasants

Angry with the Gladiators ... Those that had the balls and
the gall to

Challenge the Status Quo

Those Brave Soldiers, Hero's ... Never Valued or
Appreciated

Used as Sacrificial Lambs ... Set up for the Constant
Slaughter

Of their Bodies, Minds and Spirits

Painfully Living on the Razors edge ... Minds Slashed and Turned About

Some even Ravaging and Destroying their own

Chaotically Descending ... Hell attempting to Devour them all

Cavalier was the attitude of Ignoramuses ... Junior and Senior

Cockily feeling themselves above the Fray

Until One Earthly Planet finds itself Careening between the

Polished and Glorified Attributes of a place Exalted as a Heaven

Declarations of Hate ... Explosive Fiery Proclamations associated

Darkened Skin, Children of Ham Accusations

Embracing False Sense of Entitlement, Glorifying Bigotry,

Theft of and Trinkets traded for the Enslavement of these same

Stolen Spirit Children from their own land and their own People

Chained, Dragged, Loaded as Cargo, Sold as Slaves

Mystery, History, Legends, Fiery Locations
 Entryways to the Portals of so called Hell on Earth
Fire and Ashes ... Rinse and Repeat

Corona ... Diabolical Crown ...Evil Adorned

Otis D. Alexander
"Nay Bor" by Frances M. Laveau

Your skin is transparent, your eyes are blue

I am your neighbor, yet, you stare me through

Grandstanding in your ignorance of who and what you think I am

Completely, Deliberately, Oblivious to deep emotional scars

That have been etched upon my soul

In your Arrogance, you display a vestige of a defeated rebel flag

Crippled, however, still waving in the Wind

No distorted reflections staring back at you to question your

Authority or Superiority from those shards of shattered glass

Dark Visions never vanquished paint my body

Always reminding me of who I am in this flesh

My Awakened Memories of Strong Foundations, shoulders invisible

Strong as Blacksmith's anvils ... Spiritual hands lift, soothe, convey,

Guide and Direct Me to places where I am free to stand
Enabled, head erect, not bowed ... Eyes to see those that appear to

Bore through mine, attempting to wish me away

My Spirit cannot be shackled by Yesterday's horrendous chains

Nay Bor ... I, Me and Mine are here for the Heavens duration

Paths have been trodden through swamps and along old dusty trails

Marked with blood and tears by Generations Past for those
Yet to come

Only through a Divine Order of Love, A Sheltering Grace and Enormous

Faith has there been such Strength to Endure

Nay Bor, an acknowledgement of My Humanity, My Visibility, would be

An intelligent way to start

Peace and Respect is what I desire of You ... Because that is what I extend to you

"So Long!' by Adebimpe Adegbite

No one saw the plague coming
So I took the train unknowing
I wanted to get to work
I travelled to get to York

So long!
I wish I turned back; no, I wouldn't turn back

Now home is far behind
Quarantined, family and distance bind
No contact, my way to be kind
Without choice, our safety mind

So long!
I wish I turned back; no, I wouldn't turn back

They call us "essential"
They call us "travelers"
They call us "stranded"
But -19 is a leveler

So long!
I wish I turned back; no, I wouldn't turn back

Health is wealth
No, health is politics
Who cares!
But -19 is a leveler

Otis D. Alexander

'Better' is gold
'Well' is diamond
'Over' is platinum
But -19 is a leveler

So long! So long!!
If I could turn back, I wouldn't

"The Quadrille & 7-Step of Life" by Onika M. Thomas

PAST
I

You've been fighting alongside us all this time... Our guardians...
Our guardians, even in death:
Come back.
You have given your lives for the protection of a loved one, although long ghosts.
I do not see why our power cannot create a miracle.
Please don't tell me that atonement across centuries & millennia can't be enough...

PRESENT
II

Corruption of the soul led to the present. Innocence destroyed.
While their memories were locked away: Even with their minds wiped anew & afresh:
Their true loyalty never wavered.
They never faltered in their original mission.

III

Faint echoes of voices Mustering all their strength Over many years, across time
To deliver a single message.
To meet their beloved, only to be separated Once again & once more.

IV

Fatigue of ages, eternal slumber.
"Have I died......?" (Should I have been thankful?) "No, not yet. I still have a little strength left."
Slept but still tired, Crippled but crawling Chained to the floor.
Floating in a bubble, Enduring the wrath of the curse,
Dissolution of soul, body, spirit & mind.

V

The me who has no one
And the me who has nothing Shall fade away with the wind forever.
Give me the peace I so crave.
Tell me:
Why do I need to disturb my rest to come here?

VI

Lost to degeneration...
The trap laid from youth...
Sprung to unleash a whirlwind whose
causation Blurred and,
Became difficult to ascertain.

VII

Slow deterioration of the physical,
Exhaustion that never ceases
Pining for a past long gone…
Everything is still
all right.

FUTURE
VIII

Who will understand really? Who will stand by me?
Who will hear me, & who even will be concerned?
Who will see me & look at me without ulterior motives?
Who will welcome me with open arms?
As long as I am determined & resolute, none of it will
matter.

IX

And yet,
will flames engulf all?
When the dusts settles;
When all is said & done;
I wonder: What will remain......?

X

Perhaps, we will rise again,
As we have done in the past...
But who
will be left
to sift through the ashes?

XI

And as did those
guardians of old,
I will give
my last to this
Strickened world.

Second Coming

"Old Black Men" by Georgia Douglas Johnson

They have dreamed as young men dream
Of glory, love and power;
They have hoped as youth will hope
Of life's sun-minted hour.

They have seen as other saw
Their bubbles burst in air,
And they have learned to live it down
As though they did not care.

*This poem is in the public domain

Otis D. Alexander

"I want to die while you love me"
by Georgia Douglas Johnson

I want to die while you love me,

While yet you hold me fair,

While laughter lies upon my lips

And lights are in my hair.

I want to die while you love me,

And bear to that still bed,

Your kisses turbulent, unspent

To warm me when I'm dead.

I want to die while you love me

Oh, who would care to live

Till love has nothing more to ask

And nothing more to give?

I want to die while you love me

And never, never see

The glory of this perfect day

Grow dim or cease to be!

*This poem is in the public domain.

Second Coming

"I am a slave" by Hamza Chafki

I am a slave with no owner
I am a slave of technology
I am a slave with no labor
I am a slave to the new terminology

Every now and then I am connected
Nothing to give but only getting corrupted
I swear to God to make a halt
But, I eventually, delude myself to believe 'it's not my
fault'

I am a slave with chains around my neck
I try to escape but the handcuffs are tightened with a firm,
strong lock

Otis D. Alexander

"The Second Coming" by William Butler Yeats

Turning and turning in the widening gyre
The falcon cannot hear the falconer;
Things fall apart; the centre cannot hold;
Mere anarchy is loosed upon the world,
The blood-dimmed tide is loosed, and everywhere
The ceremony of innocence is drowned;
The best lack all conviction, while the worst
Are full of passionate intensity.

Surely some revelation is at hand;
Surely the Second Coming is at hand.
The Second Coming! Hardly are those words out
When a vast image out of Spiritus Mundi
Troubles my sight: somewhere in sands of the desert
A shape with lion body and the head of a man,
A gaze blank and pitiless as the sun,
Is moving its slow thighs, while all about it
Reel shadows of the indignant desert birds.
The darkness drops again; but now I know
That twenty centuries of stony sleep
Were vexed to nightmare by a rocking cradle,
And what rough beast, its hour come round at last,
Slouches towards Bethlehem to be born?

*This poem is in the public domain.

"ALONE" by André M. Titus, II

Another morning came, and you awake alone.

You showered alone.

You prepared breakfast alone, then ate alone.

Alone for quite sometime, feeling of emptiness in your life,

but when is it going to stop? You just don't know!

You say, It's love that's making you be alone.

Well, if it's love, maybe love have to find a place for itself,

and leave my heart, because being alone can lead to the pit

of loneliness and pity for oneself. So find a place for love to

go, so loneliness can follow.

"Daddy come home, please!" by André M. Titus, II

Daddy come home, Please!
I need you to show me, How.
How to grow,
How life flows,
And most of all how to share love, give love and receive love.

When you're home. I'm the happiest child at home.
I just don't want to be happy 2 days of a week, 2 weeks of a month, 2 months of a year, or 2 years of my life.
I want to be happy every day and every year of my life.

I want for you to see me grow.
I just Don't want to hear "Son! I Love You" over a phone.
I want to see you say it, as I hear you say it. When you hug me tight, and read to me at night. Saying, "Son, I Love You, Good Night!"

Daddy, You got to treat me better, because if you don't, I'll be happy to call another man "Daddy".
  And Daddy, I need to see you home with mama to feel her pain, her anger, her tears, her fears, her prayers, her courage and her love.

Daddy every lion has a heart, and maybe your daddy was not home for you, but I'm asking you to be here for me, or this might be the last time I call you "Daddy", Bruh!

Because I want to be Happy every day of my Life, so please come home, if you want to hear me call you "Daddy" again!

Second Coming
"Hope" by André Licencier

Trying to make it through

a pandemic

Not a mimic

It's real

Crossing international boundaries

All into Florida

Waking up each day to an outbreak

Trying to break out and make it

Not being able to see your love ones

Break out

Take out

Trying to stay safe, protected in an infected

And disinfected world

ant easy

life is in a twirl

Ant so easy

With no Kids of my own to rear

But there's   no fear

Going to court through zoom

Every other month

Is a fight

to make room

for getting custody of three young ones is right

Freeing my niece and nephew from a foster care system

That's right

At my age working towards

'Cause I   ain't quirking

  Raising these young ones

Will be a highlight

Delight

Bright light

Soon they will call me dad

This is not a TV ad

It's not sad for uncle to be there

With his swag

For we care

All and all we're trying to be

Let us

Let us see

Let us all

Get through this pandemic

It is not a gimmick

Second Coming

"The Unknown"   by Vanessa Araujo

Conspiracy?

Theories still lingering

a bit!

Close to an election?

Yes, its weird

and

too much of the

unknown.

It's scary

but not fearful.

Living my life;

not locked in

with

mixed feelings

and

it's real.

True facts!

Another vaccine?

Covid is here

And coming in seasons.

Will it potentially disappear

and on to the new?

It's a new birth!

"When You Have Had It...or The Healing Power of Sunshine" by Winifred "Oyoko" Loving

When you have crashed through the ceiling of ice
Slammed head first into the tundra
When you have flown with the flurries
Eaten the icicles
Been chilled to your marrow
Careened into snow banks
Felt your tears leak frozen to your cheeks
When you have had. It. Up. To. Here.
I will arise early, and clear a hibiscus space for you
In my gentle lavender hammock
In the warmest part of my deck
While the island sleeps, I'll gather plantings
Of tenderness drippings of honeysuckle
Chamomile tea steeped in morning heat
I will spread a lair of bare longing
A sunny, yellow splendored
Bed of flowers
Edible and sweet
For your return
For Just You.

Otis D. Alexander
"This Baring land" by Nabil Eddoumi

Human life is cheap

All people sailing on a ship

They don't know where to head to

They feel in a labyrinth all

They become like a mashed puppet

Owing to the flown time bite

Everyone struggling for his own aims

To survive and enjoy his prurient whims

The destiny is black

Due to man's knowledge lack

Why the flesh is willing?

And the spirit is weak?

Till when they keep on this barren land?

When will the day come to fulfill their dreams?

Instead of waiting for Godot

And live independently without any queers?

Can't they move ahead?

Can't they realize the Eldorado

Where everyone can live in peace

And with full bliss?

"What a Waste!" by Nabil Eddoumi

These times are out of joint
Everything has turned into waste
Where the present altered to the worst
And the past is passionately regressed
Man begins to be lost and oppressed
Since hate is love
Happiness is sadness
Ignorance is strength
Failure is success
War is peace
Freedom is slavery
Autocracy is democracy
So, the future seems foreboding
If we go on uncaring
And doing things on a lip service
But we should start a revolution
Then a bloody resistance
Against all that despotic conspiracy
To fulfill one's own needs and desires
That is the main purpose
And the destiny of everybody's existence

Second Coming
"Beams of Hope" by Nabil Eddoumi

Many boys and girls get involved in immediacy
Coz their common concern is based on accountancy
Wanting to live and enjoy their extasy
And this is really what is called idiocy

Why do we become in this damned situation ?
Where everybody is almost in hallucination
And looks for alienation rather than finding a solution
Forgetting and denying all the values of education

How can we end this rubbish ?
To make it finish and vanish
Then start living without being selfish
But a life with a sense of mutual service

Everyone must use his and her search engine indeed
Coz it is what we all need and in speed
If we want to save our hearts from bleed
And to achieve and succeed everything we want to seed

"Extirpate" by Arthur Petersen

They're here to kill us:

Manipulation

Gentrification

Celebration

Classicism

Ethnic cleansing

Demonstrations

Covid-vibration

Tyranny in our faces!

Don't they have enough friends?

Just like, "it takes a village," it would take an army to unite or even tear us apart!

Hit where it hurts.

Yes, right below the belt!

Voting polls?

Do they really matter!

We know he's guilty but we voted anyway.

Don't get tired and don't fight against the wind!
Fight back like Haïti

1804

Escape the gas chambers

Germany and unlock the door

Don't carry me back to ole Virginny

that's where Nat Turner hid the key

Queen Mary

Queen Agnes

Queen Mathilda

burned down the town.

Now, in the west it's ruled by a clown

God destroyed it first by water

James Baldwin

"Fire next time!"

Things fall apart

Go down Moses!

Go down death!

door of no return

Let me in

Dubois got through

Kwame Ture went too

Maya Angelou

phenomenal

Marcus Garvey

"bye, bye, blue bird!"

Camellia Williams ain't gonna sing no more.

We shall overcome

Today

pharaoh to let my people dem go!

Second Coming

Hit the streets children

all parts of the globe

freedom rings

hope returns

in that great getting up morning

Let our lives matter!

Let our lives matter!

Let me matter!

"Self Control" by Arthur Petersen

Losing touch with reality

using common sense

being common

looking out into the world

rain just dust

Birds refusing to sing

not a care

the world

the day goes

today is Friday

means

nothing

need a way out

Exit!

Second Coming
"Vanquishment" by Arthur Petersen

If this is war am I prepared?

If so, where is my armor or heavy utility gear?

Oh, wait here comes the enemy,

I will surely ask,

are you here to kill

or is it your given task?

I was told you would surrender,

and given orders to give you blows,

but I see no conflict

or resistance just sadness and woes.

I recognized you from near

or even afar,

you seek justice not vengeance,

I leave now without a scar.

Otis D. Alexander

"Black Gold" by Arthur Petersen

When will they ever learn?

Continuing to burn bridges

and

can't walk

over;

yet always believe;

believe in self;

believe in you;

striving for unity;

searching out greatness;

fighting with the underdogs;

underdogs are the underserved;

knowing which becomes half the battle

yet still

dream;

have a plan;

deliveries;

that's black gold!

Otis D. Alexander
"Fear" by Cynthia Rochelle Hall

Fear runs near
for those we hold
dear.

Hope never leaves
us
even when fear
teases
us.

Time is spent soul
searching
Yet turmoil is
soul
lurching.

Black lives matter;
White lives matter.
Whose lives matter?
Inclusion matters!
Justice matters!
Matter has weight
and occupies space
moreover, all lives matter and each one
has a special
place.

How did we get here
anyway-

Second Coming
in good time,
a warm day,
a rare place;
on the first of May?

Nevertheless, it is not now
that I pray for peace
with greater
disturbances not only
in the Middle East.

What comes next?
Priorities dissected
New ones elected
because of a hex.

What was important
on yesterday?
With greater blessings
we will not decay.

It seems so real
and now
Impertinent.
we gathered our thoughts
for God raised the
curtain.

Lives live!
Some are lost!
They are all cherished

Otis D. Alexander
for who's the boss.
When will it end
as he intends?
He said, "Praise God for family
in addition, support
for all of my friends."

Fear will end!

Second Coming
"If We must die" by Claude McKay

If we must die, let it not be like hogs

Hunted and penned in an inglorious spot,

While round us bark the mad and hungry dogs, Making

their mock at our accursèd lot.

If we must die, O let us nobly die,

So that our precious blood may not be shed

In vain; then even the monsters we defy

Shall be constrained to honor us though dead!

O kinsmen! we must meet the common foe!

Though far outnumbered let us show us brave,

And for their thousand blows deal one death-blow!

What though before us lies the open grave?

Like men we'll face the murderous, cowardly pack,

Pressed to the wall, dying but fighting back!

"Depression" by Otis D. Alexander

I could tell
She was once a beauty
She had very high cheekbones
flaxen hair
thin lips and a long slinky
well carved body

During her day she was social-lite with
class
and
knew all the rules of
etiquette as outlined by
Emily

She cruised me and I
examined
the passive expression
that was exhibited

I
looked
her over as if she were
an exposed piece of meat

Finally she slithered
over and begged me for a
dime for a cup of coffee
in a somber tone

but as usual
I was broke
anyway

It is a period of depression
and I ain't got time for no
ho-bo
no way

Otis D. Alexander
"Morning" by Paul Laurence Dunbar

The mist has left the greening plain,

The dew-drops shine like fairy rain,

The coquette rose awakes again

   Her lovely self adorning.

 The Wind is hiding in the trees,

A sighing, soothing, laughing tease,

Until the rose says "kiss me, please"

  'Tis morning, 'tis morning.

 With staff in hand and careless-free,

The wanderer fares right jauntily,

For towns and houses are, thinks he,

  For scorning, for scorning,

My soul is swift upon the wing,

And in its deeps a song I bring;

come, Love, and we together sing,

" 'Tis morning, 'tis morning."

*This poem is in the public domain. "Morning" originally appeared in Lyrics of Sunshine and Shadow (Mead & Company, 1905).

"Signs of the Times" by Paul Laurence Dunbar

Air a-gittin' cool an' coolah,
Frost a-comin' in de night,
Hicka' nuts an' wa'nuts fallin',
Possum keepin' out o' sight.
Tu'key struttin' in de ba'nya'd,
Nary a step so proud ez his;
Keep on struttin', Mistah Tu'key,
Yo' do' know whut time it is.

Cidah press commence a-squeakin'
Eatin' apples sto'ed away,
Chillun swa'min' 'roun' lak ho'nets,
Huntin' aigs ermung de hay.
Mistah Tu'key keep on gobblin'
At de geese a-flyin' souf,
Oomph! dat bird do' know whut's comin';
Ef he did he'd shet his mouf.

Pumpkin gittin' good an' yallah
Mek me open up my eyes;
Seems lak it's a-lookin' at me
Jes' a-la'in' dah sayin' "Pies."
Tu'key gobbler gwine 'roun' blowin',
Gwine 'roun' gibbin' sass an' slack;
Keep on talkin', Mistah Tu'key,
You ain't seed no almanac.
Fa'mer walkin' th'oo de ba'nya'd

Seein' how things is comin' on,
Sees ef all de fowls is fatt'nin' —
Good times comin' sho's you bo'n.
Hyeahs dat tu'key gobbler braggin',
Den his face break in a smile —
Nebbah min', you sassy rascal,
He's gwine nab you atter while.

Choppin' suet in de kitchen,
Stonin' raisins in de hall,
Beef a-cookin' fu' de mince meat,
Spices groun' — I smell 'em all.
Look hyeah, Tu'key, stop dat gobblin',
You ain' luned de sense ob feah,
You ol' fool, yo' naik's in dangah,
Do' you know Thanksgibbin's hyeah?

Second Coming

"Ships that Pass in the Night" by Paul Laurence Dunbar

Out in the sky the great dark clouds are massing;

I look far out into the pregnant night,

Where I can hear a solemn booming gun

And catch the gleaming of a random light,

That tells me that the ship I seek is passing, passing.

My tearful eyes my soul's deep hurt are glassing;

For I would hail and check that ship of ships.

I stretch my hands imploring, cry aloud,

My voice falls dead a foot from mine own lips,

And but its ghost doth reach that vessel, passing, passing.

O Earth, O Sky, O Ocean, both surpassing,

O heart of mine, O soul that dreads the dark!

Is there no hope for me? Is there no way

That I may sight and check that speeding bark

Which out of sight and sound is passing, passing?

*This poem is in the public domain.

"Weeping Willow" by Pamela A. Jafari

It surrounds me

Like a weeping willow tree

Encapsulating my soul

Comforting me with hanging arms

That droop and feel my sorrow

Oh weeping willow tree

Protect my dreams

From the chaos

That is stealing my breath away

I can't breathe like this anymore.

Second Coming
"BLM 2" by Pamela A. Jafari

I can't breathe

I'm full of sorrow

I can't breathe

Too afraid of tomorrow

I can't breathe

My neck is aching

I can't breathe

No whites forsaking

I can't breathe

Strangling from racism

I can't breathe

From poison trump-ism

From supremacist ideal-ism

From colorized thinking-ism

From anti-gay-ism

From religious right-ism

From stuck in yesterday-ism

I just can't breathe anymore!

And all I'm trying to do

Is say Black Lives Matter, too!

Second Coming

"Pandemic Nights" by Pamela A. Jafari

I turn over every night

And there you are

Soft and tender

So lovely

Laying peacefully

On my pillow

Next to me.

I can hardly wait

To stop DREAMING

And see you again

You can't be here

So I sleep

The days always

Until

There you are again,

In the same place

This morning-

Lying sweetly

next to me

Our eyes met

And our lips

  Almost kissed

But, then

The alarm went off

And, I awoke

From yet another

DREAM

about you

Second Coming

When the hell

Will the pandemic be through!

Otis D. Alexander

"I VOTE NOW AND FOREVER" and I
by Pamela A. Jafari

I won't go out

Protest

Marches

Signs of injustice

I can't go out

Riots

Burnings

Police brutality

I refuse to go out

Flying rubber bullets

Teargas

Targeting the innocent

No! I won't go out
But!
I will fight
Raise my voice

Pray with strangers

Teach my family

I will Zoom meet

Ask tough questions

Act with playback

Meditate alone

I will participate

Vote in primaries

Remember George Floyd

All his predecessors

All who no longer breath

I'm Black and I know

Hands up, Don't shot

T raise your Pen

And I vote

Because I can

I vote for all who can't

I vote for the right and righteous

I vote to keep breathing in America

"You've been exposed" by Pamela A. Jafari

I woke up with a chill thinking

Whites Only!

That day is over and done with! Jim Crow is dead.

Died with George Floyd three weeks ago.

You no longer get to exclude me for any reason anymore

Not on my watch, and certainly, not if I know it.

We burned all the hoods and robes. There's nothing to hide behind.

Come out of the closet. Face me and talk to me

About your dirty laundry of racist bias thoughts.

Besides, we already know what you think,

You've said them jokingly and/or in anger many times before

So just be real with me, yourselves, and the world.

You've had 400 years, yes 400 years, and that's a real big number!

400 years and several of my ancestor's lifetimes

To work out your whiteness.
You can't retreat to the closet anymore

I no longer care that your thoughts are small, antiquated, and still racist.

You no longer have the privilege to hide them in all-white spaces.

That time has passed and ended in my part of America

It's time to learn to speak your truth openly and honestly to the best of your ability.

Stop being afraid. "BlPOCs ain't gonna do nothin' to ya".

We don't have time for the low life of revenge. We want a higher power of equality

So now is the time for you to take bold steps.

You're not children.

Your skin color can't protect you anymore.

You've been exposed.

"Attempting to paint the pandemic..."
by Barry Koplen

On a Blanket by Donne's Lake, I title my effort
at painting. You approve of my two figures who
encircle their basket, of my impressionist style,
brush strokes that suggest rather than display.

You point to another canvas, touch its dried gesso.
I watch, the way a poet watches an emotion
take form, notices the way it pours into lips
and eyes, how it drains away.

You offer to pose, unbutton your blouse, block the
sun behind you. I sit in the shade of your shadow.
I do not lift my brush.
I do not study your breasts.

You do not desire to be painted.
I lower my head as if at a sacred event,
as if you are a Pilgrim, safe in my studio.
Under your feet are copies of my poems

regarding the pandemic, rather than to our blanket days
when picnics of wine and berries sufficed. Our folded
clothes were pillows then. The lake held our reflection;
it trembled. On its surface,

I scribed your name with a maple stick.
Poets work, you called it, as my letters sank in the lake's
repair. I was your author then, but now
much more than those lines have faded.

"A Mirror within your heart" by Alvin Pondexter

Look at me/don't cry,

For I am that child that throughout life/a long time

You have forsaken.

Please/shed no tears,

Hold no remorse -That right you have not.

No need for regrets;

It was your choice/you gave up.

Bitter/you say I am bitter,

You know/it pains me to laugh.

It pains me/for you wish to sympathize,

For a life you know not.

I sneer at your sympathy; for it is hollow

Second Coming

As hollow as your Heart and

And just as empty!

Otis D. Alexander

"Waiting for Tomorrow" by Alvin Pondexter

Never mistake my silence as a sign of surrender to your desires and passions.

For my silence indicate that my mind and emotions are in turmoil.

It is a battle of the rational and the irrational;

The heart and the intellect.

Your present and the mention of your name, reminiscence with pictures, visions,

And moments we shared together; happy and sad,

Throw me into this chaotic arena of indecision.

And in silence I sit, while you make passionate, aggressive advances.

Your hands touch me, and feel me in places that you so familiarly know,

Will bring me intense pleasure.

Lightly, so lightly do you place kisses upon my face and neck,

Drawing me into your realm of simplistic pleasure.

Yet, within me the battle engages on.

You have fueled energy to my heart, which becomes passive to your attention.

My mind on the other hand senses this added energy, and in return,

Fortify its own defenses to encounter this embraced attack.

The siege grows, and as it grows, I withdraw from your embrace,

Withdraw to attain my own needed space.

It is a space that you have encroached upon,

Invaded, and persistently wish to remain.

You take my withdrawal as a sign of rejection, and draw back from me,

To stare in inspection.

I observed the hurt within your eyes,

Yet I resist any overt act to relinquish your despair, your discomfort.
I feel threaten to act.
Any other time I would have succumbed,

But this time I maintain my stance, my position.

Your observation of me becomes oppressive,

And I feel the pressure, it is tangible.   It hangs heavily between us.

My body aches, the pain is physical.

I feel myself compelled to reach out and comfort you,

And yet I resist.

For myself, I must!

"Time" by Alvin Pondexter

A rainy morning

Sad news,

The blues,

Bad feelings starts my day.

A rainy morning

Sad news,

The blues,

Bad feelings starts my day.

But I have learned to hold on to my dreams anyway.

You have to learn to hold on

When old ghosts come a callin.

When despair decides to stop by just to say hey, hello.

"YOU HEAR ME...I'm an I" by Cipriani A. Phillip, Jr.

What do you do when it seems no one in power will listen? What do you do when no one in power seems concerned? Are you dismissed as a historical fear-mongering hermit?

What do you do when even those who pretend to listen, through their actions or inaction, show you they really did not hear you?

What do you do when even those who is pretend to listen, through their actions or inaction, show you they really did not hear you?

What do you do when your words of warning about a thing that is happening, in a country far away, could have devastating effects on you?

How do you prevent mass numbers of well-intentioned health professionals from being thrown into their professions' Civil War/World War, with NO war-like/medical combat training that includes psychological preparation for the equivalent of non-stop carnage?

How do you prepare their families to endure the stress, anxiety, anger, frustration, bewilderment, hopelessness most commonly associated with military family separations or even more diabolical, modern day slave-trade tactics of separating foreign born/speaking children from their parents?

This is what we have asked our first responders & their family to endure with seemingly no thought of how to heal the healers & reintegrate them into their families. In the absence of elected leadership on numerous levels of government...government...government.

I, the person, STAND as my brother's keeper, my neighbors keeper, my sister's keeper, and yes, my community's keeper.

For it is this sense of personal accountability, it is this calling of personal acceptance of uplifting my fellow man particularly in time of need, that drives me...me...me...me the government to rush to help, to strategize, organize, advocate, demonstrate, and participate. For I am the nucleus of WE...WE...WE, the people in order to form a more perfect union. I take it upon myself and I find other I's like I and in so doing form a responsive government of WE THE PEOPLE.

There is strength in numbers; there is purpose in solidarity; there is progress in lofty aspirations!

There is hope that we the people, taking care of each other, and ourselves will find orthodox and non-traditional solutions to these perplexing and vexing life altering challenges!

Therefore, it is the I's vs COVID, and despite the grotesque failures of those sociopathic, empathetic, morally bankrupt elected leaders, WE THE PEOPLE...WE GOT THIS! When the final voting tally is counted, WE, the I's, will prevail...YOU HEAR ME!

Second Coming
"THE TIMES" by AcNeal L. Williams

In a world where right and wrong are subjective
Innocents murdered and guilty protected
Where who's white and who's black determines who lives
and who dies
These are the signs of the times.

In a world where black and brown skins are commodities
Billionaires get rich incarcerating our communities
Where black and brown people still Dream to be free
These are the signs of the times.

In a world where presidents praise right-wing bigots
Black and brown people drink poison from their spigots
Where a dollar is valued so much more than a life
These are the signs of the times.

In a world where impossible NEVER means impossible
Hope is undaunted and love is unconquerable
Where we fight for justice and equality for all
This is the mark of this time.

"They and We Belong to Us" by Keith Randall Knatt, II

They are the living dead,
Because concrete and cement are just a bed.
The system hands them the fake deck of cards,
But the working class just wants to mow their yards.

Society places them in the state of blame and shame,
But who sat them down at the table to help create the game?
Medical doctors prescribe them a mental prescription.

But who and what gave them the condition?
You know, as victims we talk to ourselves,
Because we have failed to honor and understand our Godly
selves.
Then, when they turn to illegal drugs,
We want to forget who really made them slugs.

Hunger is not always when they need food,
It's the want of food that brings forth the mood.
They ask for spare change,
So they can hope for another lucky exchange.
We and they have no residential address,
But the rich and wealthy just wants another evening dress.
Destitution knows no color,
But the ignorant just complain about their odor.

They are the true book of readers,
And we know they are the leaders.
We think we know all about haves and have-nots,

But the Black Man's World has been made into a hand of
locked-in knots.

We refuse the true suggestion,
Which every victim of destitution has a different situation.
We're always looking for the false lucrative,
But we just dismiss every narrative.
They cry.
We die,
Because we insist on the lie.

The true savior is Anarchy,
Because we are plagued by classism and social hierarchy.
We can't comb the incapable uncut hair,
Because society hands us the ugly bare,
Which I call the almighty grizzly and ferocious bear.

Working class and rich think they're so above,
But our brothers and sisters of destitute know false love.
A dollar does nothing but makes us the liar.
That's why we can't find the good in a righteous fire.

We're plagued with a disease,
Because we refuse to hand the lies a permanent cease.
There is a word called "tired."
Just go and ask those of us who are "hired."
And those that are hired are "really" homeless,
Because home is where the heart is, but we made it
worthless.
So, don't you dare disparage the homeless or workless,
Because they have conceptualized the "less."

We are they and they are we.

They just want the right and respect to "be."

Love them,

Because they will give the privileged the undefeated condemn.

We and I must give them an endless and unconditional adore,

Because each second, they belong to us even more.

"Ice Cream Dream Deferred" by Keith Randall Knatt, II

"Hello," we said to the lady.

I was eager like a baby.

"No more ice cream," the lady said.

I immediately had a crushed dream and almost felt dead.

"He was a very nice man. He died from Corona," she said.

The Haïtien ice cream man is dead?

I cried,

Because somebody died.

I wanted it to be a lie.

"He was a very, very nice man," she said about our Haïtien brother.

I don't want this for another.

"He will be truly missed. He was a nice man," he said.

But the ice cream man is really dead?

I cried.

I never placed my eyes upon the deceased Haïtien.

We need a Haïtien militian.

I cried anyway, even as I am composing this poetic piece.

No justice, no peace!

A hot summer…?

COVID-19…?

And no mo' ice cream…?

The Haitian brother made the ice cream,

But the lady was the other to inform us about the broken dream.

Langston Hughes said something I heard,

And it was an ice cream dream deferred.

Second Coming
"Now Tell Me That Ain't Messy!"
by Keith Randall Knatt, II

Spray paint all over the buildings,

And not enough money is the endings!

There ain't enough food to go around,

All because the folks are busy looking down!

People don't know enough words,

But we got too many birds!

Kids can't pass the third grade,

And the babies need Medicaid!

They don't want to write,

But Corona is now the new right!

They tell us to go and vote,

But they won't tell the rich man with the boat.

I want them to leave me alone,

But the student is still looking for a loan.

Antonio from Cuba thinks his name is Jessy,

And now tell me that ain't messy!

Second Coming
"The Mask" by Keith Randall Knatt, II

The mask
is now the new no ask!

We need to get to any Nation of Islam's Mosque!

The mask is mandatory,

And "they" say it's protection for the respiratory,

And even though "She" was manufactured in a laboratory,

It will forever be just one more awful story!

And I feel sorry for every Corey!

And now where is glory?

The face mask greets the death mask.

And now Welcome to the World of Mask!

It's now the new no ask.

So go run and tell,

Because this shit here is the new real nasty show and "tale."

The United system is the ultimate and only fail,
  Because we still ain't got our mail!

Now tell me that Corey ain't in need of a bail?
Why it's a very expensive cost to be a Black male?

The chinese will still do her nail,

Because she'll use the money that's supposed to be for Corey's bail!

And she could give a hell if her man is in jail

When he robbed a white bank for her nail!

So, and again,

The mask is now the new no ask,

So go run and tell,

Because this shit here is one nasty real,

And congress ain't cuttin' us no deal!

And it's understood!

So don't ask,

And put on the mask,

And all because the vaccine and cure are both movin' slower than a snail!

Corey is still waitin' on his bail,

So Corey ain't expectin' a letter in the mail,

Because the chinese told his girlfriend to do her nails!

Through it all, thank the Creator that everybody ain't pale!

But let's get one thing understood, and y'all bet' not forget it,

And I'm only gonna' tell you this one last time!

The mask is now the new no ask,

And I don't care if you got to go run and tell,

Because this stuff here is just one more nasty show and "tale!"

"Miami's 18th Avenue" by Keith Randall Knatt, II

It's another Corona Sunday
And after the Fourth of You-Lie.
I know there's a guy around named Ray.
So much Blackness just makes me want to fly.
Real soon we'll give the enemies one endless cry.
Now the weather at the moment is a little dry,
But the rain'll come again today.
And there's a little girl on the ground in such a lay.

Miami's 18th Avenue is feelin' new,
An' the lady dancin' ain't even through!
Yeah, the kids got gum to chew,
An' Aniyah wants to walk over to Drew.

They know integrity,
They know liberty,
Because this is Liberty City.
The babies don't want the tittie,
An' the kids want to get rid of the grime n' gritty!
An' no masks for the itty-bitty?
They know their Africanity,
An' we all are tired of the oppressors' insanity.

Miami's 18th Avenue is feelin' new,
An' the lady dancin' ain't even through!
Yeah, the kids got gum to chew,
An' Aniyah wants to walk over to Drew.

The lady dancin' ain't afraid of the cars,

An' she holdin' the liquor bars.
She is still dancin' like she got the stars,
An' she dancin' like she's never been behind bars!
And the city got too many cigarettes and cigars,
But everybody wants a Jaguar!
Every Melanin out here an' over younder is The Star,
Because Harriet Tubman knew the North Star!

Miami's 18th Avenue is feelin' new,
An' the lady dancin' ain't even through!
Yeah, the kids got gum to chew,
An' Aniyah wants to walk over to Drew.

Mama, why is that lady still dancin' like that?
Baby, her mama, Ruthella used her with a bat.
Mama, is she dancin' cause she hates to chat?
Baby, all these questions are turnin' you into a brat.
Mama, where is the school at?
Baby, I taught you to watch how you use the preposition,
"at."
Mama, why don't you give me a phrase using "at?"
Baby, you are getting on my nerves like a stray cat.
Okay Mama, I remember when you asked, "Where dat witch at?"

"Effective" by Muriel "Myrrh" Cauthen

Effective _____, I resign.   The
experiences I have received here should never be repeated.
In my style, I leave you with another poem entitled . . .

"I QUIT"!

I must confess
   this place is a mess.
Physical illness occurred
   because of all I suppressed.
The more years I stayed
   the more I became depressed
due to creativity and initiative
   being consistently repressed,
coupled with a lack of meaningful
   professional work
which caused mental regress.

May I tactfully as best I can
   suggest
that your supportive staff
   is really one of the best
and we are hopefully waiting
   that the leadership
will soon profess . . . to
   no direction, no organization, no foresight
and the negative petty rest.

Thanks for letting me get this off of my chest.
Peace and love to you all _____

I happily QUIT!

Otis D. Alexander

"OLD FOLKS" by Muriel "Myrrh" Cauthen

Nothing can replace
  the wisdom of the years
There's no substitute
  for experience
that erases the fears
of what is known
of time that's blown
  except the words
that can only be
  passed back
by old folks.

One can't know it all
  when life is glowing
Only years of living
  learning and growing
lets you reflect
on what was expected
and was self-directed
  truthful words
that can only be
  passed back
by old folks.

The moon is silver
and the stars are bright
I looked out my window
and into the night.

I know I must stay
and deal with my life.
I know I must stay
and suffer the strife.
I know I must stay
until I get it right.

So I said . . . I'm not sure . . .
like you too much
   feel safe with you as a friend.

So you said . . . You'll never know
if you don't try, who knows
what may develop?   Who knows
what's already here?

So i said . . . i like you too much
don't want to be hurt.

So you said, but you'll always wonder
what might have been,
how it could have been . . .

So i said, in order to truly live
one must come out of one's self
and give . . .

Now you say, i'll call you later . . .
i'll see you later
and you mean

Otis D. Alexander

LATER . . .

I like to write of making love
   while others are writing of revolution
I have given up on revolution
  because my brothers and sisters
  now want to work within the system,
    the system of
    Busing -no busing
    Education -no education
   Program money -no money.
They want to be into politics
They want to be into jobs and
  working for promotions.
They want to prove that what the
White man says,
"Stop rioting! Work within the system"
works!
Yet our brothers and sisters
wield no real political power.
Our brothers and sisters are in
  the unemployment line,
  the food stamp line,
  the medicare line,
slave line,
  Help me find a new neighborhood
relocation line,
and many, too many, are
finding the line to
juvenile court,
domestic court,

superior court, and
psychiatric evaluation
(Wait your turn please, you're number
1,000,000,003)

So i write of making love
while others write of revolution

Cause
while we are not
revolutionizing
we are fucking
Cause
we are closer to making love
than we are to
revolutionizing
We are not truly making love
But we are truly fucking

We are fucking together (Aids)
We are fucking each other (Violence)
We are fucking the other (Indifference)
and
We are fucking over each other. (Death)

"New Moon" by Julius E. McCullough

Once one recognizes the reasons destructive conditions
exist,
He is on the way to removing those conditions
From his life and the lives of others.

As what was the seventh month, now the ninth
Designed to refocus our energies,
Signaling the beginning of Fall,
September disguised as a month of new beginnings,
May leave one wanting more and more.

For September has everything to do with trusting the
universe
And surrendering to a higher power.
Oh, Higher power who looks low,
Rescue us who live beneath your September glow,
The hope that comes from the reality of the purposed new
moon,
Its diminished luster overcast world-wide to gloom.
Dims and changes its hue from reflected light to blue,
Oh, Divine power bring us to a world anew.

As in days of old when Moses asked to "Let My People Go",
The new September moon finds us proclaiming the same
release.
Our people are marginalized, ostracized, vilified, and
murdered by the police,
Sanctioned by a new Pharaoh, President Donald Trump, is
beyond belief.

A leader who does not hear the cry of all of his people,
Will deny them their civil rights and proclaim them unequal.
The September moon runs red with the dripping blood of
the African-American slaughtered.

It is our blood that drips red from the veins of martyred:
Ahmaud Arberry, Michael Brown, Terence Crutcher, Eric
Garner, Oscar Grant, Freddie Gray, Bothem Jean, Atatiana
Jefferson, Bettie Jones, Trayvon Martin, Laquan
McDonald, Tamir Rice, Breonna Taylor, Dominique White,
Walter Scott, Alton Sterling, Philando Castile, Stephon
Clark, George Floyd, and eight days before this writing,
Sergeant Damien Larmar Daniels.

It is our blood that cast a red glare over those bombs bursting
in air.
Are we to pay the penalty for our sins as Pharaoh's
lamentations did?
The Coronavirus that claims March to September's 183,000
dead,
He neglects his people's cry and ignores the medical
professional's dread.
His lack of empathy for those affected by the virus and a
non-acknowledgement of those now dead,
Would require new leadership of one who recognizes the
omnipotence of God.

With hope for our healing, to return our gloom trodden
moon to glisten white,
For man's inhumanity to man to be replaced by God's
commandment to love one another,

Therefore, "If my people, which are called by my name, shall humble themselves, and pray, and seek my face, and turn from their wicked ways; then will I hear from heaven, and will forgive their sin, and will heal their land." under a new moon. (Chronicles2: 7)

IN THE HEART

"A Bit of You Came With Me"
(An Ode to St. Croix, U.S. Virgin Islands)
by Georgette Norman

I can no longer run to the sea

                         when the weight of the world
becomes too much
My feet longing for squishy white sand between their toes
           can no longer sink into earth's softness leaving MY
print
My thoughts can no longer abandon me and fuse with the
cadence of
the ocean's roar
and
I can no longer stare into that shimmering mirror to peer at
my soul

Sweet Island, I have left you
but,
In my mind's eye
I can still stand
on Frederiksted Pier
and gaze at the distant horizon at sunset
and see
that great ball of fire slip behind ocean's curtain

I can still feel
the soft cool tranquil trade winds
caress me
cause the coconut fronds to finger the air in a ritual dance
and

Second Coming

the banana leaf to bow in reverence

I can still look
from atop a hill on Scenic Road
arms outstretched to a moon so close
I can almost scrape its face with my fingertips
and
These memories of peace
                    of solitude
            of ONENESS with nature
                with GOD
                        sustain me

I can no longer run to the sea
But my thoughts can sink into the softness of memory

Sweet Island, I have left you
But a bit of YOU came with me

"Pandemic 2020" by Neal "Panta X" Carrington

Genocide

Suicide

Blindside

Worldwide

Off de top of meh dome

I can't go home (STX)

No room to ROAM(SPACE-84 SQ MI)

Dey know we

de bomb

Dey tickin' we off

Pass me da lazar

beam

Wipe out de

wicked dem

clean!

Spooked & paranoid/I can't avoid-I

Seeing droids/woo yoi!

We rise again!

Second Coming

"Boom Bam" by Neal Carrington

Faith/ Thee Unseen
Vision of where U
Want to be

Was and what
Shall be

Discern da signs
Cultivate a vision

"I Love Living Alone, Ha!" by André M. Titus, Jr.

I used to say, I love living alone, but now things have changed.
Do you love living alone? Truly! Do you?
Things have changed like age, body, mind, living space and even time. So, Do you really love living alone?

There are several times I really think about it. I think about certain things like a morning back rub or a kiss on the neck or the sound of Good Morning, even if you had a bad night.

The sound of the pots preparing for a healthy breakfast, or you saying, "If you're late for work, don't blame me!", or the mood swings. These are some of what's missing, if you love living alone.

I hope that the day will come, that I have to eat my words, that I used to say, "I love living alone" and start say, "I love you and I hate living alone!"

Second Coming
"Zeppelins" by Nancy Cunard

I saw the people climbing up the street
Maddened with war and strength and thoughts to kill;
And after followed Death, who held with skill
His torn rags royally, and stamped his feet.

The fires flamed up and burnt the serried town,
Most where the sadder, poorer houses were;
Death followed with proud feet and smiling stare,
And the mad crowds ran madly up and down.

And many died and hid in unfounded places
In the black ruins of the frenzied night;
And death still followed in his surplice,, white
And streaked in imitation of their faces.

But in the morning men began again
To mock Death following in bitter pain.

"A Letter to Trayvon Martin from a friend"
by Rose Mary Stiffin

"Hey, Trayvon!"
Just wanted to let you know that you dodged a bullet, man!

Yeah, remember, we talked about majoring in biology to become doctors, yeah?
Well, I'm at Florida Memorial University and I got Dr. Thomas E. Snowden for Biology. Yeah, I said Dr. Thomas E. Snowden, like that E is SOOO important!

He gives you a review every week and makes you stand up in class and answer questions. UNTIL YOU GET ONE WRONG! Last week, I was there almost the WHOLE TIME until I figured how to sit back down! Just get one wrong, which I did. I said bacteria have nuclei. I know you would say, Cone on, you KNOW they don't! Yeah, Tray, man, you dodged a bullet with Snowden!

Oh, and let's not forget the Chair of the Division, Dr. Rose Mary Stiffin. Rhymes with Griffin. Yeah, man, she tells you that. She teaches organic chemistry. She asks us to study, study, and STUDY. Like we got TIME for that, bro? We here to par-tay! Yeah, dodged that bullet again, bro. You won't have to hear her talk about research, research, and MORE RESEARCH.

You have to take physics. And, Tray, you dodged that bullet again. Dr. Ayivi Huisso teaches that class. I-E-V, yeah, that's how his first name is pronounced, He's African, but he'll tell you quick that Africa is a CONTINENT, like we don't KNOW that. Then, he tells us about some country named Togo. Yeah, Togo! Funny name for a funny country!

He'll ask you, if you're late, Suh, are you IN this class? Then, he drums into us how important physics is! What? No, man, I want to par-tay! You really dodged a bullet, since you missed out on Stiffin, Snowden, and Huisso.

But you didn't miss HIS bullet, did you, Trayvon? You didn't miss that racist killer George Zimmerman's bullet, who ignored police and trailed a goody in a hoody, the white man who didn't like the black man. The man who must have hated skittles and iced tea because he shot you ONCE in the chest just for having them.

The racist man who used a single bullet to stop you from walking while black. That bullet was sure and straight.

Oh, Trayvon, of all the bullets you missed, I wish THAT bullet could have been the one.

"The Conversation" by Shirley White Smith Nottingham

"Hello."

"Bonjour," the reply I always heard made.
Today's reply, "is your television on?"

A plane hit The World Trade."
A brief conversation and a feeling
of being safe;
when suddenly an alarm and
"I must leave this place."

Good byes, good byes
Now gone forever.
Little did I know that would be the story
to be told, ending never.

Good bye!

Bonsoir!

Au Revoir!

Second Coming
"Anthony" by Shirley White Smith Nottingham

The family's joy
Since a little boy
Shared praises of joy and acclaim
For our beloved Anthony White
So talented, so bright
A dancer so graceful
He was a delight

An uncle to cherish
A brother to love
God loved him, too
He is now in Heaven above

Never since he was born
Did we think we would early mourn
A death so tragic
He has gone like magic

A son to be proud of
His life full of love
A brother to love dearly
He supported us clearly

A life to always remember
We can never forget
We shall always love our Anthony and yet

Never a day goes by that we do not cry

Or have our hearts fill will glee
As we look all around us and see
Anthony memories

"Meaning of meaning" by Nabil Eddoumi

Many people are living in squalid happiness.
They all have means to avoid sickness
Although they have no clear purpose.
This is in fact a great curse.
Their only concern is seeking sensuality,
Being the main source of all culpability,
Having the psyche with no ability,
And lowballing their self-dignity.
So, what is the solution to cease this idiocy and absurdity,
To enable man to have his own stability,
And to give everything its straight legacy
For the sake of living with integrity
That really keeps surviving the real identity?
The recipe is that one should bear in mind
Through God and in God, man can fob of fear
And discontent as he may find peace of mind,
Giving him strong immunity and spiritual serenity.
That is the ultimate goal of every human's finality
To realize and achieve the real loyalty.
It is deemed the aim of all humanity.
Then coexisting till the vacant destiny
Every human being is bound to it imminently
Coz this is the supernatural existence set by divinity.
Every creature should live in sublimity and
"independency".

Otis D. Alexander

"My Heart-rending Love" by Nabil Eddoumi

Her name haunted my soul
She made me so fool

Her face is like the moon
Shining with bloom

She was my knight
Where I suffered at night

I was so hollow
Lying on the pillow

What was my sin?
Nobody had seen

Her love was a mistake
Coz it was too fake

Now I feel better
And no matter

"When the light has gone" by Alvin Pondexter

Oh little trouble child, how I fear for you.

You walk so proudly, your head held high,

When this world tries to bring you down.

You are a strong stallion, free spirited, running wild.

You are courageous, brave; the blood of a lion, a hunter flows through your veins.

You are elusive, swift, a graceful gazelle; the light of a sage within you I see dwell...

I sat at my window and watched him as he left, him not knowing that he had disturbed, broken my tranquility. He walked into the night like a giant taking huge strides. But I could see, well at least feel him shaking inside. Yes it was more felt than seen. I guess when you become in tune with a person on more than a physical plane, you can sense things like that, and with some degree of accuracy. Yes I felt that he was troubled; troubled by his own act of survival and violence, brought on by hostile forces beyond his control.

Yeah, I sat at this window and saw him walk into the night where the mist from the fog enshrouded, enveloped his body, and the street lights heralded his passage. And I felt sad within, because even though he stepped so proudly, I felt his shoulders slump. I am near to tears, tears simply because I see a spirit, young and strong, being slaughtered, massacred, bludgeonly beaten, and yet I sit unable to aide or rescue him. I can only provide him temporary shelter, a temporary retreat from the storm that rages without.

But how long can this battle go on; how long can I see him return to the storm; how long can I sit and feel him cry; how long can I sit and feel him die? Each time he comes back it gets harder for me to see him leave. Each time the wound is worse than the last. Confusion mist within his eyes and his body twitches ever so slightly, undoubtedly on my part more felt than seen. He's troubled. With sad realization, I realize they are killing him, or valiantly they try.

Yes, I said I was near tears for him, tears of pain, but there are tears for joy. Yes tears of joy, because even though there may dwell within him confusion, and he may be troubled, I see as well feel the fighter, the warrior within.

Second Coming
"Just how long?"   by Yuri Millien

How long has it been-
COVID19?

Is it really happening
Or merely a dream?

The homeless remains
Homeless!

The hungrey are still hungry.

They moan less!

Wait, now,

Theres a stay
At home
Order.

Now, I'm feeling
Like
An illegal
Jumping across the border
After the world ends!

How fashionably late
Is this a   new trend?

Headlines reads

Otis D. Alexander
Our health we must defend-
On who?
On what shall we depend?
Having work was never here!

Where the getting   to the
Money?
New
Frontier?

Is recession a new place?

Can we go there?

Do I need a mask?

Can I live without fear?

Just how long has it been?

Second Coming
"The beautiful innocent flowers" by Hamza Chafki

The beautiful innocent flowers have lost their color
And looked faintly pale in the burning waves of summer
Their petals weakly swaying in the gloomy weather
Seeking redemption from their ill-fated bloody planter

Who knows of their existence?
They are speechless in the noisy scandal of silence
Though they strive hard to reach a compromise or an
alliance
The artificial loads want none and show only insolence

Thus, they steal the sight of the beholders
And bewitch them with the shining fake colors
As the tricky mesmerizing mirage of summers
Or the fading rainbow colors of winters

People know never of their existence,
Nor has any smelled their odor of innocence,
They will never do
The virus has truly won like a wild, furious foe!

"Spitualy Passionate" by Brandon Trent Alexander

Because of the limitation
as to whom one can be around
this period strengthen my humanity
as well as my outer and most inner passions.

I was able to measure quality time   and search for creative
methods of increasing greater moments.
Spiritually, I was already in a good place.   Not only did I
read more of the "word," I read words from the beginning
to the end.
Observaing the spiritual transition of a frat saved this soul.
Dig deeper into greater spirituality and losing them both to
Covid.
My best man transitioned
and   the others man's best!

Decisions were made.
Yes, decisions were made based on the people I loved and
cherished and those who are depending on me.   So,   I let
the dead bury the dead   by not attending rituals.
My decisions that came naturally.

And I ushered   forward by working remotely and not
pressured face-to-face.

I am not living in fear because I am face-to-place
spiritually and passionate!

Second Coming
"Fannie Lou Hamer Who?" by Linda Jones Malonson

Mississippi was a place where it was hard to live, the land where the KKK and poor Blacks dwelled. The blacks had no rights according to the whites, and that's the way it was. There was no joy, there was no peace, and there was no love. Then freedom started to rock the nation for human rights. Many Blacks died during the terrible fight. In the town where I lived, the Black men were slow to act, but a good woman stood up, and she was proud and Black.

When the time came for voting she was kicked and beaten bad But she kept on marching although she was sad
She marched to Indianola and to Jackson, my friends No one could stop her not even the Ku Klux Klan.
They locked her up in jail; they threw away the key. But the community demanded that she be set free. Fannie Lou Hamer had a dream; no one would turn aside. Like women of old, she fought with pride.

"Hear me!" She cried, "I'm sick and tired of being sick and tired! Humans have rights. We will not surrender. We will continue to fight!" She let her light so shine that all the world would see. We are all equal, and God meant for us to be free.

They called her Fannie Lou Hamer; she was a big strong woman. She filled the children's stomach. She stood for human rights; this woman was out of sight!
Clothing, food, and money came from all over the States. She would spread love where there was hate. She showed

courage in the face of danger; she emulated peace instead of anger.

She took the money; invested it in the land. She built homes for the old and the young. Now Fannie Lou Hamer is gone to God in heaven above, may her spirit rest in peace, farewell, go with our and love.

Second Coming
"Strange Fruits:
My History is No Mystery" by Linda Jones Malonson

Laid back inside my spirit, something wild comes to mind.
Listening to Nina Simone, a quiet storm, worked its way
across my spiritual horizons.
Figured out how my soul heard my moan; it was nature's
commonality, divine poetic liturgies ...
inside the pride
declining between the lies bottled up inside
craving autonomy ...
... devoured like a feast with nothing left
for human buzzards freedom clings like a leech outside the
pride

My history is written in poetic symphonies. There are not
enough instruments, known to humanity that can play my
song; it's too complex. It's too strong. It's too long. The
music will sound good, but it won't capture my essence,
unless it comes from inside my soul; where only goodness
knows ...
inside the pride
the truth caused mass insanity slavery was no myth
sold to those in poverty
bred like beasts
became the measure ...
... of their wealth
bodies freed the mind enslaved outside the pride
Laid back, inside my mind, listening to Nina Simone's
"strange fruits". A gentle breeze blew my way, and the smell
of decaying flesh crossed my face; eternal lynchings

imprinted upon the spirit, seen on a child's hungry face ---
these pictures never go away. They didn't in 1865, and today
they are still alive. At the age of six, late into the night, the
smell of feces from a lynched man's ass permeated the air;
his carcass not a pretty sight ...

inside the pride

living the concept of exclusion a product from captivity

we're still selling each other programmed thieves politicians
and weaves ...

... living unnaturally

stillborn spirits trapped in chaos outside the pride without
duress. Stop trying to indoctrinate me, to what you think you
know; you don't know shit about me. See me without
blinders. As a gift, when looking at you, blinders will be
used. Your song has been playing far too long. In our shared
human realities; you know who suffers from unequal rights,
and horrific wrongs. You are invited, to a one on one
concert, with Nina Simone; she sings my song, beautifully.

Second Coming

"Try Following This" by Linda Jones Malonson

Nine months in a mother's womb
Seventy-one years in life's cocoon
Crawling out of both too soon
Burying myself in a different tomb

The mind created time, to reverse the error, it created an infinity
With blinders on, I couldn't see, the steps it took to free me
in the mirrors, all that I could see were illusions of this me
I didn't exist, I wasn't here, just a product of a mother's fear

Sounds bouncing off my ears
Words not heard; beliefs absurd
There are no wrongs or rights
Between the two lies insight

The weed grows faster than the grass, no excuse, get off your ass
Individually, you choose, this time the "whites" can't stop you
The old is at the end of days, teaching you from the grave
"Ask; it's given, Seek; you will find, Knock; the door will open."

All things happen within your mind
Where the blind tries to lead the blind
Where your beliefs become the enemy
Fighting you so that you will never see

Otis D. Alexander

"Embracing the Emptiness" by Linda Jones Malonson

Running on empathy ...
... searching for a door into your mind
standing in line;
empathetic friends are hard to find ...
... when running on empathy

An empty vessel can be anything;
adapt to any spirit; become any illusion
play any role ...
... as it relates to the mind; the spirit; the soul
Everyone mimicking
This flesh of me, myself and I

You created me ...
... easy to have it your way
when you know what to ask for;
know what not to say when creating a friend
who understand your dialect;
knowing the meaning of equal respect ...
... what lines to cross without permission;
no partition between she, herself and why
I already know that the truth is as ugly as a lie ...
... and just as beautiful

I am everything and nothing
All things and no name
I am the elusive "Nobody."

Which is the price I pay
To become "everybody" ...
... same as you

"Let Go!"   by Argarita Johnson-Palavicini

We have to let go

of what we loved

and what we once knew.

Let go of the comfort

that seemed to get us through.

The trying days and sleepless nights

of the thoughts that try to keep us bound.

We feel like we are lost

while hoping to be found.

God knew

what was coming through the iron

door.

It is now time

for us to rise

from underneath the floor.

Rise to new beginnings, rise up from the devastation and let go of what we knew to grab hold of something new.

Second Coming

"Crisis" by Belema Josiah

Welcome to a school called

NMB
    Where everybody here acts so

crazy   It's like I'm living in a

fantasy   I see people

carelessly

    Walking by with a

dream but they're

lazy,   Why?

In their E-Y-E a gleam   of shimmering

light   How could it
be?

Because it seems like it's only me, and maybe it is to an
extent you see

The ghost in the hallways say follow me where the
dreamers
meet

But the dreams die there because its host is
deadbeat

Listen,

I'm lyrically speaking what regular eyes can't
see

Where,   Irregular lives live care

free   Give it a month or so,   I'll be back to see the

same old people, still stuck in these mouse

traps   Mouth traps, They keep us from speaking,

peaking the floors are creaking- the roof is

leaking   Holes   Everywhere you wanna

go   There's holes in your life too, in case you didn't

know   Bullets exist, even the weather man can't

predict   The things that are happening   Here

comes the cops again   "Arrest another

hooligan."   We're fooled again,

It's Armaged-don   T
he people you love turn into fel-lons
It aint only the school,

It's the community and

the people you look up to.

Everybody's getting used to the system,   cops getting shot, children going missing.

Congress got no progress

doing things nobody knows,   "Hands up! Don't

shoot!"

   As if we were their foes.   Noiseless

exterminations, that's what's occurring,   two shots in

the head and now your eyes are blurring. We're

crying blood out here, all filled up with fears, but does

the government even care. Grown folks can't read,

saying alliteration is a little Russian,   the educational

system is a little broken. It's worsening,   the people

need to start reading, and dreaming, because it's

proceeding.   Stop being lazy and doing
hazy things,   God sees you
in the dark,
                  even when you plotting crazy

schemes. But back to school, where it all

begins- teaching kids to be drug dealers, and thug

livers, potential killers live among with us. The system

is working and that's the problem- lower class gotta

live like we're the problem. Let's stop them! "If you aint
got haters then you aint popping."

That means

       the lower class stay copping,

          but minorities

stay dropping.

       "But it's cool, it's popping."

No it's not. It's only real cool until you get caught in,
America's fishing net,

       that's stained in oil and corexit,

it's a hectic life

        anarchy
with only two rules; kill or be
killed,   something they

don't teach in schools. They say it's for the people, by
the people,   but hated if I do and hated if I

don't   but I'm blessed either

way.

I'm yelling power to the
people!

Otis D. Alexander
"Will the Real Pandemic Stand Up"

by Thomas Walker II

Covid-19 presented itself with a force that has been unknown by this age of humankind before!

It has absolutely destroyed anything that I could think of as being the epitome of something I would consider catastrophic. But the irony of this pandemic is that it revealed to the world, a' Pandemic' that, we as, 'PEOPLE OF AFRICAN DESCENT,' are well acquainted with and it does not have anything to do with a biochemically lab created disease. However, this pandemic was created in man's heart and it has spread to their minds as it has been an obsession that is systemically justified through laws; supported in courts and the "verdict of by guilt" is enforced in whatever method that satisfies sadistic minds.

This pandemic has taken more unprovoked lives than any recent war known to man. This Pandemic has been predicated based on the color of a person's skin color.

This pandemic cannot be treated medically or psychologically. It has been around for more than 400 years. It is called RACISM!

I am pleased with the response that resulted from the senseless murder of George Floyd and the revelation of the prevalence of racism to people who have never truly opened their eyes to it or people who are aware of it but have chosen not to be a part of the solution. Therefore, they too, are still a part of the problem.

My greatest fear is that we are going to lose momentum and those things will go back to the status quo that each murder of a person of African Descent will once again become an isolated event and not remain the Genocidal Pandemic that it is; that it was; and that it has always been.

Drifting" by Janell Davis

What do I see in you?
Strength and Resilience!
It's what I've always seen in you.
I saw it long ago, before I knew your voice,
Before I saw the pain in your eyes.

I remember you.
Standing in the distance,
Wearing a full metal jacket, your coat of armor
Protecting your heart from vulnerability, pain and the
possibility of love.

I remember everything about you.
Strong and passionate.
Full of the vibrancy of life,
Yet fragile and searching...DRIFTING,
Longing to be nurtured, taken into the cloak of refuge.

I remember you.
Strength and resilience guided your footsteps and led you
far.
Desire, a lust for life, they keep you motivated, intrigued.
But the security of heart and mind escapes you,
Keeps you searching...

That feeling of peace and stability,
That place of comfort and safety that exceeds all
understanding...

Is it LOVE?
It's wider than the deepest ocean...that place
Taller than the highest mountain... that place

It reaches farther than the Nile...that place.

Is it LOVE...that place?
That place...is LOVE.
Strength and resilience guided your footsteps and led you
far.
Desire and yearning for the trueness of LOVE directed you
here.

Strength and resilience,
I remember you.
Frustrated and yearning,
Needing and wanting a love of your own.
FINALLY--drifting no more--strength and resilience led
you HERE.
I remember you...

Otis D. Alexander

"Fantasy" by Janell Davis

Here I am
Stripped bare.
Clad only in five inch heels and a smoky stare.
Laid out, clean cross this red suede chair.

Skin glowing, glistening
Smellin' of the finest French perfume
Smoother than cashmere,
And a single dew drop on a velvety red bloom.

I know my power
I know my worth.
It lies up and down and clean around
My full bodied girth!

What's a girl to do
'Cept daydream and orchestrate FANTASY
The sweetest taboo!

"Trauma" by Janet Darby

Trauma of a slave ship
Loose lips
A brutal master
Sinks ships

In these waters
A system built to create victims
To never speak of their victim-I-zation
Bless this nation
In God we trust
Another white man among us
What's going on?
We shall overcome
They ask us?

What do you have to overcome?
What could it be that I have done?
I just threw a rock and hid my hand
Is that what you don't overstand?

A brutal system
Without a victim
A blood filled history
Which you claim is a victory
Is not victory .

For its victims
It remains trickery
And mockery
Madness and mayhem
May them that have been denied

rise up
No longer vilified.

"IAMNOTOK" by Janet Darby

I realize IAMNOTOK
Oh no I get it and I admit it, I AM NOT OK.
There's too much hatred going on.
As I sat one day while at the beach
with some family members,
my niece's son (light of her life),
my great-nephew, ran off to get in the water,
but he is black and will remain so,
so when I saw the police pull up on him.

He is 12, and big for his age and that's not ok
for them boys sometimes.
I immediately want to be there for him;
protect him and speak for him, but I couldn't.
I was horrified because you see
I had twisted my knee and wasn't   walking well.
So I couldn't be there with him.

I realize IAMNOTOK and I couldn't breathe
for a minute because sometimes these situations
here ain't ok. I couldn't be there for him.
   I keep remembering that day ...IAMNOTOK about this.

My father was a person that stressed loving
your family and it was an all too important a
practice that we would be participating in and
   out of the house.
Family hung out, talked smack, argued
and came back together and did it again.
I'm not use to this type of madness,
this type of brutality and IAMNOTOK.

So, as killing has become so pervasive and prevalent...

165

IAMNOTOK!

When people are killed and IAMNOTOK.
I wonder about those that are affected,
the mothers, fathers, sisters, brothers,
friends and them all that are associated.

I'm sure they are not ok. And I realize IAMNOTOK
As I hear the trauma of my brothers and sisters being
killed 'by any means necessary
by police, or one of
my/their brother's or sister's
I admit ITS NOT OK AND NO,
I AM NOT OK. I can't be ok
IAMNOTOK!

Second Coming

"Is Justice Blind?" by Ayana A. Askew

The word Black Associated with a negative connotation.
The skin color involved with mass incarceration.

Black is a stereotype that people can't get around,
assuming we're a threat, hands up don't make a sound.

From Ahmad Arbery to Philandro Castile, innocent black
men who were both shot and killed.

Eric Gardner said I can't breathe,
choked to death leaving his family to grieve.

Ahmadou Diallo and Walter Scott,
were both victims of being hunted down and shot.

MIke Brown and Freddy Gray,
lifeless   bodies in a casket put on display.

They didn't think their life would end in that way.
Hunted down by a predator who searches for and kills their
prey.

But lord I pray, that their lives are worth more in heaven
than down here.
From my mouth to God's ear, no more tears.

One bullet after another piercing their skin, Time after time
this is sadly how it ends.

Trayvon Martin was only seventeen, with a life ahead of
him that he couldn't live to see.

They all had a future with aspirations and things they
wanted to be.
Black lives taken, no fault of their own,
beautiful black queens and kings that should be sitting on
their throne.
Instead they are six feet under the ground, who were buried
without receiving their crown.

Our black brothers and sisters who deserved to live,
who in the future would have so many things to give.

Life isn't fair nor is it just,
but it gets to a point where enough is enough.

Lives taken but life moves on,
without standing up for those that are now gone.

We need to give a voice to the voiceless, the ones who no
longer have a voice.
Stay silent or speak out, we all have that choice.

Silence won't protect us, stand up and stand out,
show the world what we believe in and what we're about.

If we remain silent, a chain of unexplained killings will
form,
to our people, this will become our new norm.

Another black man shot and killed who allegedly posed a
threat,
for being black they say that's what you get.

They say I feared for my life as an excuse, They shoot and
kill, their power abused.
They say hands up, don't you even move.
We do as they say,
but they shoot us anyway.

Another murder although we did what we were told,
Another investigation of a killing unfolds.

Black lives are worthless they say,
Shooting and killing our race and always getting away.
The worth of our black lives are on a linear decline.
I constantly ask the question, is justice blind?

Why should we have to fight for justice?
Justice should be for all, but they exclude just us.

The worthless minority,
it's all for the majority.
They see us as criminals and thugs,
making the assumption that all black people sell drugs.

They see us as a statistic,
a number, a percentage,
that simplistic.

The value of a life is worth more than a number or a percent,
Just because of the color of our skin, our lives shouldn't
become irrelevant.
Hearts break, you continue to take our people away.
We are no longer safe, and we have fallen for your illusion,
thinking we were free and equal which was certainly a
delusion.

We are tired of asking for what we deserve, which is justice,
which you continuously neglect to give to just us.

Everyone else seems to be just fine,
no news stories on white on white crime.

You don't get pulled over for being white,
but we do for being black which just isn't right.
While driving while black causes you to be alarmed,
when we were just driving meaning no harm.

Walking while black, Talking while black, Just being black
is a disadvantage that we have to sadly learn to manage.
Son when pulled over keep your hands on the wheel.
Don't move a muscle please remain still.

Don't reach in your pocket and don't say a word,
because if you do gunshots might be heard.

Do what I tell you and you'll be just fine.
Wait, no son, that last line I was lying.

There is no guarantee, We can do everything we're
supposed to, but that's not what the officer sees. He sees a
comb in our pocket and calls that a gun.
We aren't even protected when going out for a run.

Another excuse to fire and kill,
someone that young didn't think he would need a will.

Young boys dying at such a young age
causing our community to act in such rage.

Fatherless children, Childless mothers, Sisters who lost their
younger or older brothers.
Families being broken apart.
the list of those shot and killed, Where do I even start?

170

Twelve-year-old Tamir Rice who was just trying to have some fun
was shot and killed because they thought it was a real gun.

Little boys dying.
Mothers crying.

Our community at a detriment mourn,
our hearts are constantly being broken and torn.

We are tired of pleading and waiting to be heard,
the reasons to kill our people are just completely absurd.

The video is there as evidence for officials to take a look.
is justice blind when the truth is there in the video, but the killers are still let off the hook?

This is getting out of hand,
living in 2020,
life threatening fears for just being a black man.

We are facing an uncovered, unmasked version of the Ku Klux Klan, No longer covered in sheets,
our oppressors and murderers kill us in the streets.

I continuously ask myself time after time
is justice really blind?

Silence is over and it's time to take a stand to raise our voices together and make them hear our cries,
Help them see what is going on by opening up their eyes,
to the unjust and the unfair ways of our nation,
to change immediately and stop the crying and frustration,
of our country and our community,
time to come together and stand up in unity.

That the only way we are going to succeed In a nation full of both corruption and greed.
This is what our nation really needs.

Rally together and make this a group effort To rid this world of terror and make our lives better.

I'm calling everyone to action to stand up for each other To save the precious lives of our black, strong, and intelligent brothers. It's been a long and treacherous road,
but we must keep moving and pushing forward Until peace, justice, and equality really do unfold.

"Tú seras la de siempre" por Erick Payan
(You will be the same as always)

Si mi alma sintiera el placer
de escribir nuestro amor en un suspiro
tendria alas para volar bien lejos
y contar en un solo verso todo lo vivido.

Yo soy el mismo de ayer y de mañana
aquel que suspiraba por ti para vivir,
el de aquella ilusión fragante y bella
que tu te hacias cada noche al dormir.

Dame el beso soñado por tu boca,
el beso inspirado por tu unico testigo
y asi correrá mi pañuelo por tu cause
recojiendo lágrimas y trayendolas consigo.

En mi vaso beberás hasta embriagarte
y cerraremos ventanas para escuchar,
crecerán los mares, llorarán las nubes
y sera imposible el podernos separar.

Algun dia mis labios te reclamarán,
asi como en mis sueños quisiera tenerte,
asi mis manos te quisieran tocar.
Tú, serás la de siempre.

Otis D. Alexander

"DESNUDA" by Erick Payan
(Naked)

Desnuda, asi la veo cuando me voy,
Asi la descruben mis ojos sin pena,
Brilla su piel como un espejo,
Mi romance, lo llevo aqui en mis venas.

Alegria entre otras cosas te doy,
Triteza? Eso no existe en mi jugar,
Caminas asi como quisiera sentirte
En un mundo silencioso, en tu mar.

Tù que llegabas con frio
Y yo a cambio mi calor te brindaba,
Tù, la que siempre me.quizo,
Tù eres con la.que siempre soñaba.

Sin embargo han psado ocho años,
Ni tan siquiera por la esquina te veo pasar,
Recuerda que el tiempo por mucho que lo intente,
No lo puedo parar.

Second Coming

"The Fire Inside" by Lovel Toran Waiters

The fire you stared burns deep within
Smoldering kissing and waiting to get

Started all over again
It could happen you see at any moment in

The middle of the day early morning
Oh especially late at night without a
lot of encouragement

Here's my earlobe go
ahead and nibble and take a small bite

The fire you started doesn't need any power
it engulfs me whenever you are near

I feel it and have to control it every
second every minute in every hour

The fire you started could make a nun blush
by the things I want to do with
and to you

Just hush(shhhhh) relax lye still
allow me to show you
guide your hands if you will
to the fire inside me.

"Lord, save me" by Ronald Rodney White

They come, grow, linger, and go.
This is evolution.
It flourishes along trading routes
Just save me!

They hitch rides without pride.
No understanding?
Just lives and years to come and to go;
forced into isolation,
loneliness,
illness,
sadness, and
a bird's nest.

We separate in the mist of love;
resurfacing
for forgiveness, and
forgiveness to come.
Have mercy on me with the old, old scars
one more time.
Just somebody save me!

Milkmaids?
Our maids?
Wet nurses?
No Hurst?
Whose curse?
Just somebody save me!

Prevailing theories   are
over the oven
and into the lab;
lunging for vaccines in a dance studio;
sitting in bars

waiting for the tab in a rodeo!

In centigrade
outbreak and we break so
take a break.
Then originate
in my backyard and
give it a playmate!

In Fahrenheit
So break out
And take out.
Don't shout
But pray out!

How dare you!
Motherland's permission in Fatherland
it's not new.
I hid in the Pyramids
and searched for a cure
in Mexico or Egypt .
I knew it was near.
Just somebody save me!

Somebody save me!
save me!
save me!
He said, "Shave me!"
Just somebody save me!

Don't blame it on 5G.
The Incas been around
for centuries before me
Pyramids in Mexico
No more disco
Jack and Jill went up a hill

and water put the California fires on the table
and that's not a fable.
Humpty Dumpty had a bad fall
To eradicate my mind and spiritual my soul

Somebody just save me.
Rest of the planet!
Cover my mouth with a bonnet!
Rest on the planet!
Just somebody save me!

He blew His nose and gave life for the ark!
Little David played his harp
and my home is over Cuba.
Deep river!
Get away, get away, gone away, been away;   it's falling,
the leaning tower.
Just somebody save me!

Stop counting bacteria!
Play marbles.
Can't count viruses!
It's horrible.
Nonillion!
Your ubiquitous existence!

Out of fingers on the piano
and into San Juan, Santo Domingo
but it's everybody's business
if I play.

I can say it
if I dance it.
I can prance it.
Just somebody save me!

STORY

Thelma and Nephew by Fred Motley

It was the worse snowstorm they'd had in six years. Her children wanted her to go home and rest. But she couldn't leave her husband in the hospital. They had an oxygen mask on his face. The doctor told her his chances were fifty - fifty. something clawed deep inside that her husband was dying. She shuddered and quickly blotted that out of her mind,

She looked at her son who was looking out the window, and thought how it was a terrible snow storm the night he was born. The midwife had gotten there somehow. It's amazing how nothing seems to stop midwives from coming to deliver babies. Maybe it's because they are bringing life and they traveled with angels.

Her husband, his eyes closed, knows she is by his side. He can't speak or move, but he prays to live for he doesn't want to leave her alone. Yet he feels his time is near because he is remembering things he hasn't remembered in years.

During their forty years of marriage, there had been heartaches, cussing, slaps, and separations, but they always came back to one another. Why just last week, he got on

179

her nerves so bad she told him to get out and don't come back. Now sitting beside his bed in the hospital she prays he lives for she doesn't want him to leave her alone.

She had loved him from the first time she saw him. Still they have not said I love you to each other in thirty-seven years. She didn't because he made her so damn mad not telling her he loved her. He wanted to tell her but he always got embarrassed. So, he acted like the words did not matter.

After all, a man didn't go in for all that mess. Why did he have to tell her he loved? He married her, didn't he? They had nine children and he came home every night! Didn't that show he loved her? That's what made him so mad with her, always wanting him to say he loved her. Now he wished he could tell her "I love you I have always loved you."

He needed to say he was sorry but his speech was gone. Everything came out in grouts and muffles. Maybe she could see his thoughts in his eyes. He opened his eyes. He noticed she had grown very pretty. A little plump but, at her age and all he had put her through over the years and the children, she looked good. He hoped she could see it in his eyes. As the doctor lifted his hand, she saw how frail he was. Living with him day in and day out, all these years she never noticed him aging.

She looked at her hands and instantly touched her hair. Did she look old and faded to him? She had long forgotten to think about her looks. When she looked in the mirror, she didn't look for prettiness, youthfulness, she looked for neatness. She likes perfume and uses it regularly. Now she wondered how she looked to him.

When they were courting, she fussed about how she looked. She would comb and press her hair with Royal

Crown; wash and lotion her entire body, then spray Avon's Midnight Blue perfume on lightly, put on Red Fox stockings and last she put on her favorite lipstick, Passion Red by Avon. Funny she would think of that right then.

She was smiling. He thought she must know he is trying to tell her how pretty she is. He reached out his hand; he wanted to touch her face. She moved in closer. "What do you want?" She grabbed his hand, he kept pulling her closer. She ended her face close to his to see if she could understand. He lifted his hand and touched her face.

It had been much too long since he touched her face, but not too late he thought. She placed her hand on top of his hand and held it tight to her cheek. She pressed her bronze lips into the ashy white palm of his hand. His hand is cold, she thought. Her lips are warm, he thought. He wanted words to come out of his mouth. He could smell "Midnight Blue" perfume.

The doctor called her and their son into the hallway. "We will keep Mr. Nephew overnight. His vital signs do not look good. If there are any changes we will call you. Please, just go home and rest.' he said.

She put her coat on slowly, got her purse, and kissed him on the forehead. She hadn't kissed him in nearly thirty some years. Her lips felt soft on his forehead. He reached for her hand. Why hadn't he held her hands more often, why hasn't he kissed her lips more often?

He kept trying to pull her to him, mumbling something she couldn't understand. "What do you want?" she asked. "I can't understand." His eyes were begging don't go! "I'll be back tomorrow. The doctor thinks I should go home. You'll be fine." he wouldn't let go of her hand. He was trying to tell her something. "What?" she asked. "He wants you to kiss him again." their son said.

She kissed his forehead passionately. He remembered the first day he saw her some forty years ago. She was the prettiest woman he had ever seen. Her hair was shiny and thick, down on her shoulders. her skin was velvety black, smooth and clear. Her lips lingered on his forehead. She felt embarrassed when she opened her eyes. She was blushing like a schoolgirl.

He held onto her hand as she moved from the bed, until only the tips of their fingers touched. Their son, his arms around her shoulders walked her out the room. She was moving but it was like she was standing still. Love memories danced through her soul as midwives and angels echoed to her heart to turn her feet around.

"Momma what's the matter? Where are you going? Momma!" her son called to her. Watching her walk down the hall he could see, really see what love looks like. Perhaps love will be the midwife to make it through the snow storm and bring life and angels this time. Outside, the angelic white snow continued to fall from the black midnight blue sky.

HOPE

"Meditation Class in the Time of Pandemic"
by Helen D. Laurence

Sit comfortably with a straight spine, head and neck in alignment.
Inhale.
Om, shanti shanti shanti.
Om, peace peace peace.

Ask yourself: What is my motivation for meditation?
For example, you might say, To experience Awakening. Liberation. Enlightenment. To activate the neurotransmitters in the brain that engender spiritual experience. To feel the interconnectedness of all beings, and understand that we share the same origins and are made of the same star stuff that was present at the beginning of the Universe. To dwell in the understanding that we are all One, as in this exchange between a student and the spiritual teacher, Ramana Maharshi. "Questioner: How are we to treat others? Ramana Maharshi: There are no Others."

Or, you might say, To meet challenges with equanimity. You might have faith that establishing a regular meditation practice will help calm your reactivity to the inevitable, as in Yogi Amrit Desai's response to a student in 1986 in St. Croix. Amrit had said we should love one another without exception. The student asked, I'm involved in a seemingly arbitrary and malicious lawsuit. How can I love the guy who's suing me? His response: "You don't have to love

183

him. Only, just don't hate him, because that hurts you more than it hurts him. And be grateful for these difficulties, because they prepare you for that which we will all encounter - death of a loved one, fatal disease. *After all, we're all just waiting in line...* "

You might want to meditate in order to develop Compassion. In the Tibetan Buddhist tradition, compassion is understood as the source and essence of enlightenment, and in fact as the primary purpose of our life here on earth. You might want to practice developing compassion by directing loving kindness first to yourself, and then outwards in widening circles - to a benefactor or someone who has been good to you; then to a neutral person such as a casual acquaintance; then to a difficult person such as an enemy; and finally extending compassion to all beings everywhere. A loving kindness practice might sound like this: "May you be free from danger... May you be happy... May you be healthy... May you live with ease."

Your motivation for meditation might be To prepare for Death. Mine is. Something happened many years ago that convinced me of the necessity of being prepared for death. (*"After all, we're all just waiting in line..."*) I was in Massachusetts and my father in law, with whom I was very close, was in St. Croix. He was in treatment for cancer, but I did not know he was dying. This was 40 years ago, so there was no texting, no instant communication. I was studying in the library, finished and walked home. As soon as I closed the door behind me, I had the powerful feeling that someone was trying to break in. I knew it was irrational, but it was very intense and frightening. I called my husband who was in Texas at the time, and told him about this. He said I should just make sure all the doors and windows were locked, which I did, but the feeling persisted. Finally, I got into bed, and when I turned off the light and closed my eyes, I saw fearsome visions of green and yellow demons in

184

kaleidoscopic whirling motion. I pulled the covers over my head and prayed. Finally, I fell asleep. The next morning, my sister in law called and said "I'm sorry... Dad died last night." Years later, I read The Tibetan Book of Living and Dying by Sogyal Rinpoche, who describes the "forty-two peaceful and fifty-eight wrathful deities" depicted in the Tibetan Book of the Dead. "This is a vision that fills the whole of your perception with such intensity that if you are unable to recognize it for what it is, it appears terrifying and threatening. Sheer fear and blind panic can consume you... (p. 277)." I like to think my prayers helped my father in law through this fearful phase in the process of his dying. More recently, my mother died at the age of 104. She was at the bottom of a long, slow slide into dementia by then. The hospice nurse called me when Mom was dying and when I arrived, she was struggling mightily, flailing violently with her fists as if striking out against unseen assailants. I leaned close and whispered encouraging words, but she battled on, until a shot of morphine was administered, and her struggles ended.

Ask yourself: What is my goal for today's session?
For me, the goal is simply, To follow the breath for 10 in-breaths and 10 out-breaths, without distraction, and to be present at the final breath. This is much harder than it sounds. In our minds there is the constant chatter of planning, remembering, wandering, fantasizing. As soon as you realize your attention has wandered away from the sensations of the breath, congratulate yourself for achieving that "aha" moment of realization, and gently, without labeling or judgement, return the attention to the breath.

Have no expectations. There is no such thing as a bad meditation, as long as you diligently return the attention to the breath, despite the inevitable distractions. Take a moment to consider some potential distractions... Politics,

Facebook, shopping lists, Covid19, books, TV shows, movies, interpersonal drama, health, illness, snacks, laundry… the distractions are endless. Let them come. Let them be. Let them go.

Adjust your posture.
Straight spine, head and neck in alignment, tip of the tongue touching the roof of the mouth, just behind the front teeth. Let the shoulders drop. Do some neck rolls. Eyes closed, or open and softly focused on a spot on the floor in front of you. Relax.

Bring your attention to the outside (traffic noise, drone of distant planes, wind, birds, people in the street…).
Then, bring your attention to the inside (hum of the fridge, clunking of the AC cycling on and off, ambient buzzing and creaking of the house).
Bring your attention to the sensations of the breath in the body; the abdomen and chest rising & falling.
Bring your attention to the sensations of the breath at the tip of the nose. Focus your awareness on the cool air coming in, the moment of suspension between the inhale and the exhale, the warm air going out, the moment of suspension between the exhale and the inhale.

Relax.
Enjoy.
Observe.
Let it come, let it be, let it go.

Inhale.
Om, shanti shanti shanti.
Om, peace peace peace.

"Letter to the Next Generations" by Jeffrey Dean Swain
Dear Family:

I woke up alone and crying some days ago, overwhelmed by the horror of the moment that George Floyd's death and how it had had compelled people into the streets. My well-cultured faith could not afford me solace against the anger – yea, the rage - I felt against our enemies or against the fact that you too had witnessed the wholesale taking of black life is trivial. I could not make sense of the carnage seen on television: a black man's life oozing out of him as he wailed to a dead mother who could help no more than the desperate citizens standing around as he drew his last fainting breaths. How many times had black people watched one of us die at the hands of white authority and could not physically intervene for fear of their own deaths? I lost myself in that moment because I love you so deeply, more than I have ever articulated out loud. I thought of you and wondered how I would feel if that knee had been on your neck.

Many of you (my nieces, nephews, cousins, friends) I only knew as children, and some of you I never met or held a conversation with; but you are always been on my mind. Everything I have done in my life was to help you know that you can fashion the dreams you want because I did. Life is never perfect but it can be shaped and molded despite the barriers you face. You can bend it to your will because others have done it; and the fatalism fed to black people about accepting the limits of life is the sustenance of fools who would have you believe God created you only to fall in the rut of subservience or dependence and stay there. In reality, He made you without boundaries; but life can hem you in as you grow and learn and are told that certain paths are off-limits to you but open to others. I tell you do not believe or embrace the lie of limitations. I am still aspiring to do more now after four college degrees and six published

187

books and after authoring 15 or more doctoral dissertations generated out of my own mind. And I still have not done my best work or achieved my highest ambition. I urge you to bend life to your will and God will push back barriers.

There are some things I want you, the next generation, to know about this world we inhabit. Age changes perspective and I am older, not necessarily wiser, and have seen more. I am nearly sixty now and have come to the realization that the world is not much better. We're told we've "come a long way" because slavery is not our present lot; but I see slavery and its ghosts everywhere in American culture. Slavery has transmogrified itself; but it still cuts into the skin and burdens the body so that we cannot run as far as we want. I have watched us – just a few generations removed from our enslaved ancestors - fight to be recognized as humans who are valuable outside ourselves. I have seen the courts abandon us. I have seen us struggle against invisibility. I have seen politicians – even black ones - be modern days Judases who trade our lives for pieces of silver. I have seen law enforcement try to beat us into submission – something we will never embrace. We are a rebellious people who have always lived free. That should not change.

What you see going on around you is the deconstruction of the myth of America and the unveiling of a country that has never loved your blackness. America cannot fathom how we of the African diaspora have survived, lived, loved and thrived despite all their attempts to kill us. They have tried to obliterate us in the Dominican Republic. They have conducted programs against us in Argentina and Peru. They hunted us down and turned our skins to wallets in Australia. After lynchings in America pieces of our bodies were taken as souvenirs. In this one death, you see the face of hatred incarnate that every generation before you struggled against with all their might. I don't want to understand white people. I think it a waste of life force to attempt to reason about their malicious acts toward black people. I don't think we need to have talks to explain our pain because they are the authors of our tears. They have had at least four hundred years to know us and to repent what they've done. I don't want to understand what compels them to kill or to build the machinery of society that efficiently does it for them because I don't have a mind that wants to hurt others; so, I could never comprehend what drives their evil. I will not make excuses for whites who were not alive before 1865 to commit acts of injustice or for those who presently benefit from the seeds planted by their ancestors. I wonder why we keep trying to rescue white who say awful things against us and apologize when their purses are threatened. There is no integrity in such apologies. Think Drew Brees, the quarterback. There will be no thinking of the Confederate flag as anything but a badge of treason and a symbol or our oppression, not some glorified remembrance of a proud or honorable southern heritage. I do not feel empathy for those who benefit today from the racism that impacts every aspect of our lives. Neither do I appreciate their smug condescension at the lot of the poorest of us.

Who are these people? They are you enemies. Even the best of them would rather benefit from your disadvantage rather than give up their privileges. The most liberal of them have their limits for what they will sacrifice for your uplift. The most religious of them believe God made you inferior to serve, be less intelligent, bear their burdens, and live in dirty rather clean spaces. The nicest of them would rather not live next to you or have their children sit with yours. They constantly imagine a world where they do not have to encounter you on equal terms. Moreover, they would prefer a world without you. Do you know that America is more segregated now than before 1970 and that 80% of white people do not encounter a black person for the first time until they are in college or at work? This means that for nearly the first 18-20 years of life, they may never encounter a person of color directly. Imagine what that means if they only understanding of black people is generated by television. Don't ever be anyone's "black friend." All white people are not evil but they all collectively benefit from our exploitation.

My family began in the Carolinas (Paternal - North Carolina and Maternal – South Carolina). I have traced us back to 1795. That's 19 years after the founding of America. My father's name was Albert (1914); his father was Frank (1885); his father was George (1848); his father was Henry (1821) and his father was Jethne or Jethro (1795). That's just one line of my heritage. You need to know your tree. The late Betty Wright was my cousin via Isabel Swain, my grandmother who married Frank Swain. Betty Wright's grandparent was a sibling of Isabel. I met Betty and one of her brothers who lives near me and we discussed this. My DNA profile is 37% Nigerian, 35% e Congoan/Cameroonian, 11% from Mail, 7%, Senegalese, 4% Benin-Togo, 4% Ghanaian, 2% English/Swedish. This means I am 98% African and probably you too. We have Africa in our blood. This is no myth. Both lines of my family (Albert, my father, through North Carolina and Frances, my other, through South Carolina) have roots in slavery. There are many textures of beauty and achievement in my family that need more exploration. Be proud of who you are. There are no non-First American people in America who have paid more to be here than black folk.

Black folk in America, having worked for free as slaves, are today owed as much as $17 trillion dollars according to the New Your times (P. Cohen, 2019). This debt remains unpaid. There is a precedent for reparations. The Japanese received compensation for their World War II involuntary interment. You have every right to be here, more so than most Americans whose families immigrated later. You are children of the African diaspora, the spread of black folk from the continent – both involuntarily and voluntarily. Our efforts for freedom and civils rights forced America to be better. We are the impetus for "a more perfect union." Every civil rights movement subsequent to our for women, suffrage, LBGTQ rights, Latinos, immigrants, gun rights, conservatism, and more have patterned themselves after our efforts. Even still, once achieved, many join our enemies in voting against our interests and openly disdain us.

The stain of American racism can limit your dreams. We have all been tainted, injured, and abused by it; but we are still here. I wrote my first book (Black and Still Here, 2003) because I was literally surprised that we have survived as a people and as families. Just think about this. We survived slavery. We survived the codification of slavery into law, making our ancestors slaves for life. We survived the 3/5ths Compromise that gave Southern states the right to partially count us so that white southerners could have more representation in Congress. We survived the 1857 Supreme Court's Dred Scott decision that declared us property and not citizens. We survived the abolition of slavery (1863 [Emancipation Proclamation] and 1865 Amendment), a fight for equal protection under state laws (1868), and the fight to vote (1870). We survived Reconstruction and the rise of Jim Crow segregation and the violence of the insidious Ku Klux Klan and malicious White Citizens Councils. We survived Plessy v. Ferguson (1896) which formalized separate but equal public accommodations, Brown v. Board of Education (1954), Emmit Till's death (1955) and the year-long Montgomery Bus Boycott (1957). We survived the destructions of Rosewood, Florida, Elaine, Arkansas, and Black Wallstreet

191

in Tulsa, Oklahoma. We survived being undereducated, overtaxed, and underrepresented by Congress. We survived being redlined into the poorest, most decrepit neighborhoods. We survived crosses being burned at our churches and homes. We survived *Slavery by Another Name* where Douglas O. Blackmon showed blacks were still being enslaved until World War II. We survived more than 4,000 documented lynchings and many more undocumented. We survived professional sports teams that rejected our best athletes until it was too economically ridiculous to continue the practice. What you saw in the death of George Floyd was a re-enactment of the deaths of tens of thousands of us whose names will never be known. Some of those names were possibly the same as your last name. Yet, we are black and still here.

Embrace blackness, not African-Americanness. We have gone through a number of name changes from Africans to blacks to Negroes to Afro-Americans to African-Americans. We've consistently been called niggers throughout. I prefer blackness because it connects us to all Afro-descendant peoples in the world who live in the Middle East, Asia, the Caribbean, Latin America (150 million), Europe, America and on the continent itself. Don't listen to fool hearty black folk who deny their blackness or Africanness because they want acceptance. There will always be people like Candance Owen and Ben Carson and Kanye West who'll articulate white hatred with black voices, calling us shiftless and unambitious. People can choose their own race but they cannot choose the DNA passed to them by their ancestors. We are Africans living in America. Thinking of ourselves within only the African-American confines cuts us off from black folk changing the world everywhere. Cuba is more than 70% of African descent; so is Brazil. There are many blacks who would choose to be called anything but black because of the lighter color of their skin, the loose or straight texture of their hair and the grey or blue color of their eyes. Among Latinos/Hispanics, there is a joke about "the black granny in the closet" which notes that some of them hide their African heritage. When you hear mestizaje, moreno, zambo, pardo, cafusco, maroon, quilombo, mulatto or other terms, these are Afro-Latino folk to whom you are connected in Cuba, Mexico, Peru, Haïti, the Dominican Republic, Argentina, Colombia and elsewhere. Many Latin American countries have a battery of other names for people of African descent without calling them black.

What is racism? It is a choice whites have made to deem themselves superior to every other people. In 1452, a Papal Bull or edict was issued by the Vatican that permitted Portugal and Spain the right to enslave people in the name of Christianity. These two countries, strangely, led the European surge into Africa to capture and export slaves to their own countries. Their history with Africa pre-dates the existence of America or its former colonies. Ironically, the Moors of North Africa invaded and ruled the Iberian Peninsula (Portugal and Spain) from roughly from 700 A.D. to the 1400s when Ferdinand and Isabel of Spain came to power. Just think about this. After 700 years of intermixing with the Moors and the Portuguese and Spaniards, Africa is later enslaved by their mulatto cousins. Other countries in Europe eventually joined the onslaught. In 1884, the Berlin Conference on colonization, convened by Germany, Turkey (i.e., the Ottoman Empire), Austria-Hungary, Belgium, Denmark, Spain, France, Italy, the United Kingdom (England), Netherlands, Portugal, Russia, Sweden-Norway, and the United States, met to partition Africa and make it easy for them to exploit its people and resources. King Leopold of Belgium is said to have been responsible for the massacre of more than 10 million people in the Congo for the rubber trade although he never went there. His government-funded mercenaries would go into villages and kidnap women and children, then compel the men to harvest sap from rubber trees. See the cartoon of below of Cecil Rhodes after whom the Rhodes Scholarship and Rhodesia (now Zimbabwe) were named, which depicts European hubris. Notice he is standing on a map of Africa. Africa is still recovering today and remember that African nations only gained their independence from colonizers in the mid to late 20th Century.

Racism is also based in a belief that God has given one people the right to dominate all others. That belief led to the subjugation of Africa, Asia, Latin America, the Caribbean, the Middle East and all other non-white regions to impose their will by force. The British used to say, "The sun never sets on the British empire." Why African and Caribbean nations still welcome visits from the Queen and her scions is a mystery to me. Even today, the Chinese are exploiting Africa to feed itself and to obtain mineral resources. A new holocaust Is beginning.

Depending upon your source, 12 to 20 million Africans were taken by force into western slavery. Henry Louis Gates, Jr., in his book *Black in Latin America (2011)*, puts the number at 12 million. This dissemination of Africans around the world does not include the Arab (eastern) slave trade, which operated from approximately the 7th century into the 20th century and is alleged to have taken away another 17 million black souls (New African, 2020). It should be noted that the Arab slave trade preceded the European African slave trade and was just as ruthless and money-driven. We rarely think of both of these as detriments to Africa but both used our labor, exploited our ancestral lands, vilified our culture, destroyed our historical records, disparaged our languages, and sold our bodies for money and repaid nothing. Try not to commodify (reduce to mere numbers) black slaves but think of them as humans with families who were cut off from their heritage, cultures, languages, lands, and bereft of knowledge of themselves. Most of you know nothing Ghana, Mali, Songhai or Great Zimbabwe. Hence, the African diaspora or spread of black people throughout the world was so great that there are very few places we cannot be found. Of course, through voluntary movements from Africa, the Caribbean to Europe, Canada and elsewhere, we have further expanded our presence. Please note that our languages, music, and cultures were never lost. They were suppressed but never exterminated. Our music is in Cuba and all of Latin America. Jazz, the only original America music, came from us. Our languages were blended with the languages of enslavers and colonizers but they never died out. Think about the creole and patois dialects of the Caribbean. Still, one thing that holds true in all places is wherever we are found, darker skin affords you worse treatment, economic status, quality education and physical abuse and death. Even in the modern slave trade of some 27 million people worldwide, Africans are still being sold in places like Libya. The world has had no empathy for dark skin outside Africa. It still doesn't.

Racism is sin. *The Bible* does not condone racism. The belief that God is pleased with racism is a fabrication of white Christians who lifted up "slaves obey your earthly masters" (Ephesians 6:5, Colossians 3:22) or Paul's direction to the slave Onesimus (Philemon, 12-14) to return to his master. One of the worst misuses of *The Bible* was in the conquest of African and the domination of other peoples from Hawaii to the Philippines to Puerto Rica and Haïti by America. The Word says we're all made in the image of God (Genesis 1:26-27), owned by God (Psalm 24:1-2), fearfully and wonderfully made by God (Psalm 139:14-16), and children of God (Galatians 4:7). White people like Carl Von Linne and Johanne Blumenbach set up a hierarchy of color and assigned levels of intelligence and civility with light skin at the top black skin at the bottom. Do not be naive in faith. Any religion can be misused in the name of profit. Neither Islam nor Christianity is exempt. James 4:17 says, *"Therefore to him that knoweth to do good and doeth it not to him it is sin."* This passage covers the sin of omission. Whites knew it was wrong to enslave bodies but their distorted faith allowed them to kill millions whose blood still cries from the ground.

Racism in inherent in capitalism. Do not think capitalism or money is a savior since our understanding of it based on the American ideal of wealth which requires the exploitation of the "least of these in society." America, since its inception, has counted on the mistreatment and manipulation of the poor as the foundation of its economic structure. Remember, that indentured servitude of whites and blacks helped to build the colonies pre-American Revolution. As the country grew, a shortage of labor led America to codify slavery into law, first in Virginia (1662) and later in other states like North Carolina where laws were passed making slavery permanent for anyone whose mother was a slave. In fact, slave laws developed through the 1680s, even noting that being a Christian did not make a slave free. Slavery was set aside at the Constitutional Conventions but again codified in the 3/5th Compromise that defined us as valuable for representation in Congress but not as citizens. We were not citizens in America until 1865. Even with full citizenship, equality has been denied. These ideas permeate American culture to this day – that blacks are not equal. So, even Europeans who were not considered "white in Europe" (Irish, Italians, for example) have adopted the mantle of "whiteness" and a disaffection for blacks as the platform for their accumulation of wealth and the denial of wealth to us. Dark skin folk can't pass. We do not have the luxury of being "Americans" as long as our skins marks us for "otherness." The mask of conservatism has become a synonym for acceptable racism. These are the folk who employ the Southern Strategy of fear-mongering every election cycle. These are the folk who claim "law and order" as they cheat us and kill us without punishment. These are the folk who built walled communities with restrictive covenants to prevent homes being sold to us. These are the folk who vote against laws that would cure police brutality. These immigrants decry new immigrants public then hire Mexicans and Latin Americans secret to exploit their labor and women. These folks want to make America great when it never has been that for us.

Never fall for the idea that merely working hard and accruing wealth separates you from the poorest black person in America. Four college degrees (B.A., M.S., J.D., and PhD) and six published books, two Cadillacs, a house with a pool, and disposable income have not made me exempt from economic exploitation or potential death at the hands of police. We get "policed" while other communities get served. We get charged more for insurance and more interest for loans. We get less investment in our communities and stores like Publix are still absent in black enclaves like Liberty City and Carol City although we generate a trillion dollars for spending in the American economy. There is nothing about the money-generating process in America that does not rely on the exploitation of people of color – blacks especially. Despite the success of athletes and entertainers, racism is built into the infrastructure of entertainment, music and sports. The reason black artists formed their own record labels is older artist where cheated. Little Richard, Ray Charles and others broke away and formed their own companies to produce their own albums and records. We still struggle again white power in the distribution of records.

Entertainers like Monique, the comedienne, and Isaiah Washington break the rules when they speak out against white actors and entertainers being paid more for the same work. This is still true to today if you take note of professional football and basketball which rely upon the skills of blacks (70% plus in each league) to make billions annually. Neither sport truly honors the contributions of its players because they continually overlook blacks for coaching and executive positions. Although they play players hundreds of millions individually, they reap rewards of billions annually. The professional drafts should remind you of slave auctions dressed in better clothes but rich white men still bid for the best talent as poor black athletes line up to be examined and show whose the strongest and fastest among them. There is one black majority owner, Michael Jordan, in all four major sports. The only way you become an owner is for the white guys to vote you in. Remember as well that entertainers and athletes are our one percenters (1%). They are aberrations not the standard. Not every young black child will succeed in those arenas. Most of us still need and education of some kind. Your mind is your most valuable asset.

Racism is destructive. The impact of racism is not just economic. It has health consequences as indicated by our poor health outcomes with heart attacks, strokes, diabetes and high blood pressure. It has mental health consequences. We have been slow to acknowledge the post-traumatic stress of racism and economic deprivation. Every time there is an unjust black death at the hands of someone white, we go through trauma. Just think about the anguish we all have felt in the past four weeks trying to digest the death of George Floyd after listening to his pleas while a white officer dispassionately squeezed the life out of him and government officials had to "evaluate" whether those officers should be charged with the lowest forms of murder.

198

We grieve and withdraw and teach our children the limits of blackness after every event, saying "just come home alive." We generally believed it was premeditated and deliberate. Who did not say, that could have been me! My earliest encounter with race was from a white neighbor in Liberty City in Miami when my white playmate who lived next door called me a "nigger" and ran into his house. At seven or eight years old, I knew what he meant. I have been stopped by the police and asked: is this your car (Mercedes); where are you going; didn't you see me; and why are you in this (wealthy) neighborhood? While I was an attorney, I was handcuffed, thrown in a police car, and encouraged to lash during a traffic stop. The officer opened the door as I laid on my side, having never been arrested or handcuffed, struggling to sit up and asked me to kick him. I had graduate college students disbelieve I was their professor or be surprised I as black at teaching at Barry University. I was asked in court was I really a lawyer or the defendant? I have been questioned about my credentials as a PhD and asked by white people to park their cars while waiting for my own. This happened twice in Aventura. In law school at the University of Miami, I was told I did not have the technical ability to draft legal documents, implying I should quit. The implication was I did not belong there. My legal writing professor did not know I had graduated as a Phi Beta Kappa in English and majored in English in graduate school at Atlanta University before law school. I later beat her best white student in Moot Court competition. I have been challenged as to whether I could write and publish my own books. When I applied for high ranking jobs in Miami-Dade Public Schools, I was told by a member of the selection committee - a relative by marriage - that when I left the room, jokes were made about "what made me think I was qualified for such jobs." I generally had more degrees than the people interviewing me. These are a few just my racialized experiences. They are too numerous to name.

I am certain that you, too, have had some. But imagine what this does to the mental health and the psyche and feeling in the pit of your stomach every time a police car rolls up behind you. Imagine the multitude of microaggressions not mentioned we have endured and think about how they erode self-confidence, plant seeds of doubt, and make us question ourselves. It is no coincidence that young black people talk about not expecting to live past their twenties or expecting to go to jail or shunning educational opportunities when educators in their schools plant the idea that we are not smart. This is how racism destroys, angers, and seeps into the being of black people. Inferiority is meant to be absorbed; however, you don't have to drink the Kool Aid. Think about the destruction it has caused when we still do not think dark skin is beautiful even though we have all shades in our families. I know the truth of what I speak, having taught literature, and criminal and constitutional law.

Although this sounds more like a diatribe than a letter of love, I do love you and regret that we've not been closer. I spent my earlier years seeking the American dream and neglected my ties to you. I regret that. Those were the years when you were coming of age and maturing. I apologize. Still, I would have you benefit from the wisdom of age. There is something about seeing more years behind than in front. I want you to know that you come from a great family with a fierce streak of independence. I want you to know that none of what I described has ever stopped us from living full lives. I want you to k now that the people who survived slavery and segregation did it for you and you must not let what you see in front of you convince you that your life can be limited. It is my hope that this letter will be passed to future generations or that you will generate your own so that we may know that God did not condemn us to the bottom rungs of life. We, too, can live where we choose, achieve what we desire, and thrive to whatever heights we are willing to work and aspire.

I don't want you to wake up in tears as I did a week ago, burdened with the idea that change has not come when a black man's life can be stolen on film and people have to wonder did he deserve it?   Even if I don't know your name, I love you and want the best for you.   Fight and never quit or give up. Fight to your last breath.

Again, I love you.

Otis D. Alexander

"Remembering Ms. Beah Richards: Centennial Reveals Her Life and Legacy to be More Timely than Ever" by Dinizulu Gene Tinnie

"Who?" That is probably the first word that comes to mind for upwards of 90% of Americans reading this headline. A select few who are of a certain age might recall Beah Richards' Oscar-winning Best Supporting Actress role as Mrs. Prentice, the mother of Sidney Poitier's character in the 1967 blockbuster movie "Guess Who's Coming to Dinner."

However, in ways that might never have made hers a "household name," the extraordinarily talented child who was born Beulah Elizabeth Richardson 100 years ago this year on July 12, 1920, in Vicksburg, Mississippi, would grow to become not only an acclaimed actress of screen, stage, and television, with nearly a dozen significant Hollywood movies to her credit, but also an important playwright, poet, author, and a boldly inspiring, fondly remembered mentor to younger artists.

However, in what might be called her greatest role of all , Ms. Richards, much like her own mentor and friend the legendary Paul Robeson, did not allow stardom and show business to deter from her more compelling commitment to being a fearless and tireless, dedicated and outspoken activist for social justice and equal rights for peoples of color worldwide, and for women and workers in general.

It was in this role that she closely followed the nationally sensational case of Willie McGee, a Black man in Mississippi accused of raping a White woman with whom he apparently had a consensual relationship, for which he had gone through two mistrials and was going before a third jury in 1951, when Ms. Richards, reflecting on the whole history of the South where she was born and raised and which she knew only too well, penned a brilliantly insightful poem entitled "A Black Woman Speaks, of White Womanhood, of White Supremacy, and Peace," reproduced below, which might be considered a lasting emblem of her lifelong creative genius, sincerity, courage

Space here does not allow for the full exploration of her many achievements that they deserve, but readers are strongly encouraged to research and be inspired by her remarkable life, one of so many that have mattered so deeply to the making of this country without the recognition that is due.

The centennial of Ms. Richards' birth on July 12 is a most appropriate occasion to give her memory that overdue recognition, perhaps with some gesture of remembrance in our homes, or mention of her name in our places of worship on that Sunday, but certainly by recognizing how acutely timely and relevant her poem is to the present time, as the attention of the world is focused on Black America's dual plight of suffering a grossly disproportionate death rate from both the COVID-19 pandemic, and from a rash of incidents of unwarranted police brutality, as protesters and observers around the world denounce the blatantly racist Trump administration in aiding and abetting these outcomes.

The poem becomes even more timely today as a presidential election approaches and we are reminded, of the astonishing 2016 "election" of Donald Trump, in spite of having actually lost by some 3 million popular votes, due to the American technicality of the Electoral College, and the startling role of the 53% of White women who voted for a self-avowed misogynist and racist, and against the nation's possible first female president (compared to 94% of Black women voting for Hillary Clinton).

In the wake of #MeToo, impeachment, COVID-19, and other developments in thus Year of Awakening, the world will be watching America's White Womanhood even more closely than Ms. Richards did in 1951.

On the brighter side her legacy, we must recognize LisaGay Hamilton's brilliant 90-minute 2006 HBO biographical documentary "Beah: A Black Woman Speaks" (taking its title from the poem), a recent screening of which inspired a group of viewers to launch a nationwide effort to commemorate Ms. Richards, between July 12 and September 14, the 20th anniversary of her death at age 80 in 2000, with articles, programs, film showings and virtual activities at both grassroots and official levels, that will bring to light her many contributions and those of people whom she inspired.

What better way to begin our next 400 years of history in these lands than by celebrating and elevating the memory of those whom the last 400 years of history so routinely excluded, ignored, misrepresented, and denied.

Beah Richards' (1951) classic poem follows:

For my known and unknown maternal and paternal Black Women ancestors who both slaved and worked (for barely livable wages) in White folks' homes for centuries...

A Black Woman Speaks...
Of White Womanhood

Second Coming

Of White Supremacy
Of Peace

It is right that I a woman
black,
should speak of white womanhood.
My fathers
my brothers
my husbands
my sons
die for it; because of it.
And their blood chilled in electric chairs,
stopped by hangman's noose,
cooked by lynch mobs' fire,
spilled by white supremacist mad desire to kill for profit,
gives me that right.

I would that I could speak of white womanhood
as it will and should be
when it stands tall in full equality.
But then, womanhood will be womanhood
void of color and of class,
and all necessity for my speaking thus will be past.
Gladly past.

But now, since 'tis deemed a thing apart
supreme,
I must in searching honesty report
how it seems to me.
White womanhood stands in bloodied skirt
and willing slavery

reaching out adulterous hand
killing mine and crushing me.
What then is this superior thing
that in order to be sustained must needs feed upon my flesh?
How came this horror to be?
Let's look to history.

They said, the white supremacist said
that you were better than me,
that your fair brow should never know the sweat of slavery.
They lied.
White womanhood too is enslaved,
the difference is degree.

They brought me here in chains.
They brought you here willing slaves to man.
You, shiploads of women each filled with hope
that she might win with ruby lip and saucy curl
and bright and flashing eye
him to wife who had the largest tender.
Remember?
And they sold you here even as they sold me.
My sisters, there is no room for mockery.
If they counted my teeth
they did appraise your thigh
and sold you to the highest bidder
the same as I.

And you did not fight for your right to choose
whom you would wed
but for whatever bartered price

that was the legal tender
you were sold to a stranger's bed
in a stranger land
remember?
And you did not fight.
Mind you, I speak not mockingly
but I fought for freedom,
I'm fighting now for our unity.
We are women all,
and what wrongs you murders me
and eventually marks your grave
so we share a mutual death at the hand of tyranny.

They trapped me with the chain and gun.
They trapped you with lying tongue.
For, 'less you see that fault-
that male villainy
that robbed you of name, voice and authority,
that murderous greed that wasted you and me,
he, the white supremacist, fixed your minds with poisonous
thought:
"white skin is supreme."
and therewith bought that monstrous change
exiling you to things.
Changed all that nature had ill you wrought of gentle
usefulness,
abolishing your spring.
Tore out your heart,
set your good apart from all that you could say,
think,
feel,

know to be right.
And you did not fight,
but set your minds fast on my slavery
the better to endure your own.

'Tis true
my pearls were beads of sweat
wrung from weary bodies' pain,
instead of rings upon my hands
I wore swollen, bursting veins.
My ornaments were the whip-lash's scar
my diamond, perhaps, a tear.
Instead of paint and powder on my face
I wore a solid mask of fear to see my blood so spilled.
And you, women seeing
spoke no protest
but cuddled down in your pink slavery
and thought somehow my wasted blood
confirmed your superiority.

Because your necklace was of gold
you did not notice that it throttled speech.
Because diamond rings bedecked your hands
you did not regret their dictated idleness.
Nor could you see that the platinum bracelets
which graced your wrists were chains
binding you fast to economic slavery.
And though you claimed your husband's name
still could not command his fidelity.

You bore him sons.

I bore him sons.
No, not willingly.
He purchased you.
He raped me,
I fought!
But you fought neither for yourselves nor me.
Sat trapped in your superiority
and spoke no reproach.
Consoled your outrage with an added diamond brooch.
Oh, God, how great is a woman's fear
who for a stone, a cold, cold stone
would not defend honor, love or dignity!

You bore the damning mockery of your marriage
and heaped your hate on me,
a woman too,
a slave more so.
And when your husband disowned his seed
that was my son
and sold him apart from me
you felt avenged.
Understand:
I was not your enemy in this,
I was not the source of your distress.
I was your friend, I fought.
But you would not help me fight
thinking you helped only me.
Your deceived eyes seeing only my slavery
aided your own decay.
Yes, they condemned me to death
and they condemned you to decay.

Your heart whisked away,
consumed in hate,
used up in idleness
playing yet the lady's part
estranged to vanity.
It is justice to you to say your fear equalled your tyranny.

You were afraid to nurse your young
lest fallen breast offend your master's sight
and he should flee to firmer loveliness.
And so you passed them, your children, on to me.
Flesh that was your flesh and blood that was your blood
drank the sustenance of life from me.
And as I gave suckle I knew I nursed my own child's enemy.
I could have lied,
told you your child was fed till it was dead of hunger.
But I could not find the heart to kill orphaned innocence.
For as it fed, it smiled and burped and gurgled with content
and as for color knew no difference.
Yes, in that first while
I kept your sons and daughters alive.

But when they grew strong in blood and bone
that was of my milk
you
taught them to hate me.
Put your decay in their hearts and upon their lips
so that strength that was of myself
turned and spat upon me,
despoiled my daughters, and killed my sons.
You know I speak true.

Though this is not true for all of you.

When I bestirred myself for freedom
and brave Harriet led the way
some of you found heart and played a part
in aiding my escape.
And when I made my big push for freedom
your sons fought at my sons' side,
Your husbands and brothers too fell in that battle
when Crispus Attucks died.
It's unfortunate that you acted not in the way of justice
but to preserve the Union
and for dear sweet pity's sake;
Else how came it to be with me as it is today?
You abhorred slavery
yet loathed equality.

I would that the poor among you could have seen
through the scheme
and joined hands with me.
Then, we being the majority, could long ago have rescued
our wasted lives.
But no.
The rich, becoming richer, could be content
while yet the poor had only the pretense of superiority
and sought through murderous brutality
to convince themselves that what was false was true.

So with KKK and fiery cross
and bloodied appetites
set about to prove that "white is right"

forgetting their poverty.
Thus the white supremacist used your skins
to perpetuate slavery.
And woe to me.
Woe to Willie McGee.
Woe to the seven men of Martinsville.
And woe to you.
It was no mistake that your naked body on an Esquire
calendar
announced the date, May Eighth.
This is your fate if you do not wake to fight.
They will use your naked bodies to sell their wares
though it be hate, Coca Cola or rape.

When a white mother disdained to teach her children
this doctrine of hate,
but taught them instead of peace
and respect for all men's dignity
the courts of law did legislate
that they be taken from her
and sent to another state.
To make a Troy Hawkins of the little girl
and a killer of the little boy!

No, it was not for the womanhood of this mother
that Willie McGee died
but for a depraved, enslaved, adulterous woman
whose lustful demands denied,
lied and killed what she could not possess.
Only three months before another such woman lied
and seven black men shuddered and gave up their lives.

These women were upheld in these bloody deeds
by the president of this nation,
thus putting the official seal on the fate
of white womanhood within these United States.
This is what they plan for you.
This is the depravity they would reduce you to.
Death for me
and worse than death for you.

What will you do?
Will you fight with me?
White supremacy is your enemy and mine.
So be careful when you talk with me.
Remind me not of my slavery, I know it well
but rather tell me of your own.
Remember, you have never known me.
You've been busy seeing me
as white supremacist would have me be,
and I will be myself.
Free!
My aim is full equality.
I would usurp their plan!
Justice
peace
and plenty
for every man, woman and child
who walks the earth.
This is my fight!

If you will fight with me then take my hand
and the hand of Rosa Ingram, and Rosalee McGee,

and as we set about our plan
let our wholehearted fight be:
PEACE IN A WORLD WHERE THERE IS EQUALITY.

"Wizardry" by Barry Koplen

Even if Zellner recalls Bloody Monday in Danville, VA,
I won't ask him about its brutality. Don't have to; I know
local leaders, Reverend Campbell, Reverend Echols,
their children. I know about the beatings. And the beaten.

Main Street, where they marched, didn't part like a Red Sea
for protesters although their blood reddened Main. That
cruel day, I, an insignificant Jew, saw terrified young
blacks, jittery white cops anxious about administering dour
strictures familiar to their parents, their parents' parents.
That day, no one asked me to impersonate Moses although
I knew the motions, had seen pictures, his raised hand, its
commanding staff, his steady eyes. Zellner didn't try to be
Mosaic, probably wasn't born knowing how. But that June
10, 1963, Main Street wore a speckled banner: *Social
Injustice Lives Here!* It died that day. With each bludgeoned
marcher, with each bloodied baton, another prejudice
dropped like a broken chain on stiff asphalt.

Segregated movie theaters, public schools and libraries,
color-coded restaurants began to disappear. Without much
help from me. Sure, I was there, but my voluminous notes
and Holocaust pictures, locked in my trunk, didn't matter.

I sensed that Jew-hating was different from black-hating so
I didn't say much. Still, decades later, I'm waiting for my
chance to march, waiting for a Zellner to call to say he's
coming again to Main to start something, something big
enough to cancel anti-Semitism at its source.

Someone like Zellner would probably do that for us Jews.
He would likely say it's way past time for that.

Of course, he'd find me first to make sure things were done the right way so that profound change would take hold, would last. He'd take me aside like a co-conspirator, would ask me about that Red Sea trick, about the wizardry he'd need to pull it off.

"A Ministry of Hope" by Blair E. Alexander, Sr.

Over the past several weeks we have all been impacted by the graphic and horrific scenes witnessed on our televisions, in some of our neighborhoods, and certainly on our streets. These scenes of unrest, turmoil, and disorder have caused us to take a deep breath, to take a seat and in many cases to take a knee and pray. Consequently, we must remember that the work of the church is always accomplished through the hands and the hearts of the body of Christ; the people of God. When "faith is the substance of things hoped for", we must be the substance and the hoped for, so that the world will see our faith.

During these times when so many young activists are doing the heavy lifting by protesting in the streets, organizing rallies in their communities and speaking theirs and our truth to those in power, we must join the fight in meaningful and measurable ways that support and strengthen the cause for justice, freedom, and most importantly love. In chapter 10 of the gospel according to Luke, in the story we know as the Good Samaritan, when the young lawyer asked Jesus who is my neighbor, the lawyer was indeed shocked to find out that his neighbor in the story was not a person from his faith, his clan or even someone that looked like him. Like many others have defined over the years, the lawyer limited his idea of neighbor to those in his circle, his synagogue, and near his home. The lawyer did not fully consider and understand that his neighbor could also be someone from another faith, another community and even another race. This story always reminds me of a quote by Alan Turing, who shares "Sometimes it is the people no one can imagine anything of, who do the things no one could imagine."

This seems to be a good time to continue reminding the world of the love of Jesus Christ and to offer "A Ministry of Hope" by doing the things that no one could imagine while being the substance of things hoped for in our neighborhoods. In other words, let us join in the fight by showing and sharing kindness, joy, hope and love in our community. In addition to the wonderful acts of kindness we currently engage in, here are a few other tangible ways we can participate in the protest for love and unity in our community:

- Provide cul-de-sac care packages of tissue and paper towels to those in our neighborhood.

- Show random acts of kindness by paying for the meal of the person behind you in the drive-thru line.

- Drop off a case of water or a bag of food to a family member, friend or neighbor.

- Continue making care calls to family, friends, and others.

- Financially support organizations fighting against injustice.

- Continue providing support to local food banks.

- Let someone know you are praying for and with them.

Dr. Martin Luther King, Jr. reminds us that "In the end we will remember not the words of our enemies, but the silence of our friends." Let us endeavor never to be silent or silenced by the bigotry, prejudice and intolerance of others.

Instead, let us commit to opening our hearts, our minds, and our mouths to ensure our voices of hope and love are heard throughout the land.

Otis D. Alexander
"The Slave Bible" by Blair E. Alexander, Sr.

A few days ago I had the opportunity to visit the Museum of the Bible (MOB) in Washington D.C., and to see one of its newest exhibits. It is an exhibit on "The Slave Bible," a book officially entitled Parts of the Holy Bible, Selected for the Use of the Negro Slaves, in the British West-India Islands. The Slave Bible, on loan to the MOB by Fisk University, a Historically Black College and University, is an edited, and redacted version of the Protestant Christian Bible. It was developed by a British Missionary Society specifically for slaves living in the British controlled West Indies Islands such as Barbados and Jamaica. Although the British Missionary Society's intentions were to teach slaves to read and write and to proselytize or convert the slave's religious ideas from those of their native lands to Christianity, they also wanted to maintain slavery for Great Britain's economic causes.

According to the research accomplished by the staff of the MOB, the developers of The Slave Bible, undoubtedly people of religion, deliberately and intentionally erased and removed 90% of the Old Testament and 50% of the New Testament so that slaves would hear, understand and believe that slavery was sanctioned by the will of God. Therefore, stories about Moses and the Exodus of the Hebrew people towards freedom, or the story of Joseph the dreamer and his rise to power in pharaoh's house, were omitted together with stories from Galatians, which state, there are neither bond or free, and that we are all one in Christ Jesus. These compelling stories are missing because they represent Biblical heroes who fought to free their people from tyranny and oppression. Many times the Bible is used to liberate, to restrain or incarcerate people. The story of The Slave Bible is an example where one race knowingly misused, misappropriated and misinterpreted the Biblical text and acted as a rogue agent for their God of money, power and control to restrain and constrain another race for financial and economic gains.

Therefore, it is always up to us to be the scholars, theologians and historians that must uncover, recover, and in many cases discover the truth, so that all men and women are set free. Edmund Burke said it best when he shared, "The only thing necessary for the triumph of evil is for good men to do nothing." Let us have the willingness and the courage to combat evil with love and knowledge and commit ourselves to always doing something for the cause of hope and justice. Be well, be blessed, but always be vigilant.

Otis D. Alexander
"Hope" by Adebimpe Adegbite

Reasons to despair:
No out, just in; stay in
No run, just walk; walk in
No shout, just talk, just whisper; whisper in

None knows
When this shall pass
When all shall be well
When friends shall embrace
And hugs be widely spread

Hope:
In the company of family
In the unity in struggle
In the fight to overcome

Hope:
When families die
When friends are ill
When we are unsure

Hope in doubt!

Still we rise
Like the Phoenix
Right from the ashes

Though masked in fear
Fear being sanitized

Second Coming
Sanitized to reach out
Out in our world
World of uncertainty
Uncertainty!

Still we rise
Like the Phoenix
Right from the ashes
Singing Hope!
Hope!!
Hope!!!

"Resting to Run" by Catherine I. Williams

The World Health Organization declared Coronavirus (COVID-19) a major concern on January 30, 2020. A few months later, on March 11, 2020, it was announced that it was a pandemic. Then came the shutdowns, lock downs and hunker downs. I called my Father and asked Him to please lead, guide and direct me because I was filled with anxiety before the pandemic, and now stress increases with each passing day. The busyness of my life, the clutter, and everything around me were taking a toll. I was frustrated because I wanted to do something to help front line responders, victims of COVID-19 or "something" – but what? I, myself, was a mess! My Father said, "My child you need to rest, take some time to rest in me." (Matthew 11:28-29)

"Come to me, all you who labor and are heavy laden and I will give you rest. Take my yoke upon you and learn from Me, for I am gentle and lowly in heart, and you will find rest for your soul." (Matthew 11:28-29)

Because I hear and heed my Father's voice (John 10:27), I knew I had to do something. I needed to work one myself before I could help front line responders, victims of COVID-19, or help to meet any of the prevalent and rampantly growing needs.

What does rest mean from God's perspective? Why should I rest when everything and everyone around me seems to be actively doing something e.g., helping others, marching, protesting, etc.? How do I rest?

Rest, from a secular perspective, means to cease work or movement in order to relax; it includes quietness, tranquility, unwinding and taking it easy. Rest from a biblical perspective, according to Vine's Concise Dictionary, "is not a rest from work, which is part of a secular definition. Biblically, it is rest in work, not a rest from activity, but the harmonious working of all of the faculties and affections, of will, heart, imagination, conscience – because each has found in God the ideal sphere of satisfaction and development". Resting from God's perspective, coupled with some scriptural imperatives, lead me to use my time during COVID-19 to examine my ways, all aspects of my life, and make sure that I am in compliance with God's will, ways and purpose for me. I needed this time for a spiritual self-analysis, recovering from the inadvertent trappings and busyness of the world which causes anxiety and the stress that Satan was using to try to take me out! I had to put in a lot of time and work – blood, sweat and tears.

My rest started with a spiritual self-analysis which included a mental introspection and reflection of: the direction I'm heading in (Is it right?); the changes and adjustments I need to make; role ambiguities and or clarifications that I need to realign and refocus; and what God wants me to do for His Kingdom. This required emotional honesty.

Resting became a spiritual discipline, and I had the Holy Spirit to guide and coach me to do a lot of work (still in progress) which may also help others:

• Extensive daily praying (1 Thessalonians 5:16-18)

• Daily studying and doing God's word (2 Timothy 2:15)

• Meditating (Joshua 1:8)

- Releasing burdens – giving up worrying, reasoning and Anxiety

- Relying wholly on the Lord (Proverbs 3:5)

- Learning to give God the glory in everything that I do (because "I can do all things in Christ…" (Philippians 4:13)

- Maintaining peace because God is in Control (Isaiah 35:4)

Having faith and knowing that God is always with me helps to refresh and relax my mind and body. I am now RESTING TO RUN, "preparing to press toward the goal for the prize", (Philippians 3:14), do what I can to help those impacted by COVID-19, and or serve wherever the Holy Spirit directs me to. I will run to do that!

Second Coming

"The Day the COVID-19 Demons Visited Me"
by Andre M. Titus, Jr.

On Wednesday, March 18, 2020, it was a cool night in Corona, Queens, New York, when my body began to feel this fierce heat.

Was it the heat of horniness? Oh Snap! Coronavirus is all around my community. Could it realy be Corona?

I slithered into the kitchen and prepared a hot cup of Honey Ginger Tea with garlic, followed by cold shower and retired for thee evening.

Next morning, I called my sister and shared the experience of the a hot night. She said, "Bro, I got you."

Yes, if that was the sign of the devil COVID- it's gone. I still called my doctor and told him that petrifying evening, and he said, "Go get yourself some Tylenol and Robitussin and call me should there be a change. However,Do Not Go to the Hospital!"

Several days later, I received a package that fill with natural herbs and homegrown of leaves - Lemongrass, Sour Sop, Mint and Sugar Apple, soaps and vitamin tonics. I was armed to fight the COVID Demons!

The calendar flipped as days went by as I prepared my body and mind by consuming natural herbs and homegrown remedies. I was fine until Sunday, March 22, 2020. However, slightly after midnight, I heat resurfaced and this time it was the Coronavirus heat and it came with the COVID19 Demons to take me down.

Fever - so hot. I felt like a Fire Dragon that everything I touch, I burnt. With "no one" to call for help, all I could hear was the echoe of my doctor saying, 'Do Not Go to the Hospital!"

So, I ran for my rubs, herbs, shower, and everything possible. Suddenly, I stood still and spoke with God. I shouted out "Lord, am I the chosen? Am I supposed to suffer and carry this enemy coronavirus to save my family and friends? I'm read!"

The fight was on for weeks on end; battling the loss of appetite; tasteless foods; cotton throat; skirmishing for air to breath at night; weakness, and the little physic I had dematerialized to skeletal.

The"Will to live" was the determination to tell - to tell you about the struggles of loneliness, isolation, patience, and the power of prayer.

With siblings, family members, and friends praying for my healing, had given me more of determination to make it through this coronavirus fracas..

I asked myself a few questions: Why am I here? What can I do to change things in my life? Where do I begin? Who should I seek? And How will my life be beneficial to humanity?

The turning point came after weeks of fighting coronavirus - a severe cough attack overpowered my lung for two hours; causing repetive coughing and shortness of breath.

The phone rang and an Angel was sent to talk me through this cough attack. Believe it or not, after the Angel prated and prayed with me as the cough disappeared unknown to me. I emerged and tried to cough, however, I could not produce a sound. I felt a hunger in my stomach, so I dragged myself to the kitchen. I started preparing a meal not knowing if I were able to taste it or eat it, since I had not eaten in weeks. As I placed the first spoon of food into my mouth, the taste of the herbal butter sauce on the cornmeal ball was the taste of the sweet thing. I will never forget, that I ate four bowls non-stop!

At that moment, I knew the answers to my questions the Day the COVID19 Demons visited!

"Reflections and Hope" by Freddie Barnes

I secured myself in a small office inside of the headquarters building of 2nd Supply BN-Rein on AL-Taqaddum Marine Corps Base in the Anbar Province of Western Iraq in the spring of March 2008. The exact date was March 18, 2008. It was about 10am Iraqi time when candidate Barak Obama gave his momentous speech on race, "A More Perfect Union." It was "One Shining "and defining moment for candidate Obama. Many would say he clinched the presidency with his speech. He certainly won my vote.

I could not contain my level of enthusiasm and pride as President Obama spoke. It was hard for me to keep from calling attention to my whereabouts with exuberant shouts and high fives into thin air. I felt so much pride as a black man and proud to be an American—even more so being in uniform.

For the eight years Obama was president, I never felt prouder to be an American. He was not a perfect president. He made some colossal failures, in my opinion. For example, I believe his signature legislative achievement, health care, was far too costly for his supporters for the gains/benefits won. Health care continues to be a major impediment to many Americans. States have some role in the lack of health care for all Americans, for sure. However, Obama's signature legislation had more gaps and holes in it to be a likely option for many Americans.
I believe Obama caved into Republican defiance when he wanted to alert the Nation to the Trump campaign being

assisted by Russian influences. Personally, I believe he should have used his bully pulpit to alert the Nation despite Republican objections and obstructions.

Despite the wins and losses of the Obama presidency (no different from other presidential administrations), he was, however, someone who made you proud. He represented the office of President without any need to offer excuses or justifications for his excesses or gaffs, or egocentricities. Obama's great gift was making everybody he encountered feel special and appreciated, from the janitor to the lunch counter server. "The man was dope!"

I offer this reflection on the Obama presidency because I am a proud American. I am a retired military officer. I work and pay taxes like many Americans. I am proud to be an African-American. To be sure, I am privileged that my children have been reared to share the same purview.

Look at where we are. I cannot begin to articulate or convey the level of my disgust, outrage, and horror with the current White House (WH) occupant. (I struggle to refer to him as President.) President Trump is wantonly corrupt and shameful. For almost the last four years, I have felt less proud of being an American.

Trump has been on the record of saying he does not care that he does not represent all Americans. I know I am in that excluded group, as are other peoples of color. As inarticulate as Trump often is when he speaks, he is very eloquent when he boasts about his followers (known as his base) at the exclusion of most/all others. In the words of the late Barbara Jordan, "I too am an American."

Now I do not spend my nights wishing for Trump to include me in his version of America. Trump does not represent anything about this country. He has elevated the corrosive nature of unchecked power and celebrated the shameful acts of cronyism, nepotism, demagogy, and incompetence. His sins as president are many. From caging young children to inviting foreign influences into our elections for which he was impeached. Compounding matter is the onslaught of a once in a lifetime public health pandemic that this president has completely botched the response to the COVID-19 pandemic. To be sure, Trump would not be so cavalier and out of control if it were not for his Republican enablers.

Congressional Republicans continue to "wink and nod" to all the excesses and grotesque behavior of this president—jeopardizing our pre-eminence as a world power as well as our stature as a free and democratic people. It is clear that the Republican Caucus made a Faustian deal with Trump to ignore his excesses and narcissistic, self-serving behaviors while he co-signs on their slate of judges to fill vacancies on the Federal judiciary. This culpable and scandalous behavior are not only dangerous but also offensive to most Americans.

Some proud Americans, like myself, actually went into "harm's way" to defend the country that is now being pillard and degraded by a narcissistic executive and a compliant

Republican caucus. All the talk around our revered documents, the Constitution and Declaration of Independence et al laws, are nothing more than hollow words on paper that clearly have lost the awe from those who put up with this behavior without significant checks and balances.

The United States is in significant decline here at home and via image around the world because of Trump. The country is also a very dangerous place to live, if you are a person of color. The rise in hate violence inflicted on people of color is alarming. No, Trump did not sign an order for such conduct. The president given tassel approval and license to purveyors of hate and intolerance through his rhetoric and policies. His down talking to those entrusted with the defense of our internal and external borders (FBI, CIA, military) when they do not accommodate his whims. I am embarrassed when senior military leaders and seasoned intelligence officials cave in to him. When Trump is silent on the most blatant and outrageous conduct involving racial intolerance and violence is a not too secret signal to those who would seek to traffic and peddle in racial and racist acts and propaganda. To my mind, the man in the Executive Office is the titular head and sower of division and racial hatred that could very easily lead to a war between the races. This, regrettably, seems to be his plan. He makes no apologies or excuses for his nillhism and utter contempt for humanity and the rule of law. Frankly, Trump is trying to demoralize the electorate to foment enough hostility that it will result in electoral apathy and swing the 2020 Election to him by default. That, my friends, cannot happen.

As a preacher, I am "duty bound" to offer another alternative/hope. I see some irony in all of Trump's "mess." His excesses and demagogy will force conscience white people to voice their disapproval. For far too long many sympathetic whites sat silently and watched the abuses black people and peoples of color endured under white supremacy and years of racist policies. Too often, sympathetic whites were not willing to "rock the boat" regarding speaking up.

Black people and other people of color usually gave voice to their oppression. Some modest gains were won. However, systemic racism and white supremacist strongholds persists. This time is different, I believe. Something shook a moral nerve in all people of conscience and good will when the world witnessed a white police officer pinned his knee on the neck of a handcuffed black man until his life was squeezed out of him while three other officers observed as though this was "standard operating procedures (SOP).

It is an arduous task not to be morally shaken to see a murder carried out in such a public way. By virtue of witnessing this crime makes it almost impossible to avoid taking on the very system that is responsible for such a crime. The voices calling for a change to this system are not black folks only but a chorus of multicultural voices demanding change, not just for white repression of black people and other people of color, but an end to the excesses of the current administration.

I believe something else is occurring in the country. There is no question that a post Trump presidency will require a lot of repairing. Trump has taken a hammer to many of the institutions that foster and protect our democracy. He demonstrates contempt for voting rights, the rule of law, and the prerogatives of Congressional oversight, to name a few. He has pilloried the protectors of our internal and external defenses such as the CIA, FBI, military and other defense agencies along with the complicity of the Republican Congress. Yet, the American democracy is resilient.

For example, my financial planner always calms me in tense financial times by saying the markets are resilient. We have some recent history to acknowledge this. During the 1980s, at the end of the Reagan Administration, the country was spiraling from the Savings and Loan (S&L) Debacle.

During the George W. Bush Administration, the country went through a stifling recession, which was the result of too much spending on wars and tax cuts causing the federal treasury to become financially anemic.

The good news is that these economic declines were reversed because of some corrective financial policies and the resiliency of the markets. The point being that this country, albeit flawed and imperfect, has enough of a solid foundation and infrastructure to reconstitute itself and revitalize its badly weakened democratic institutions.

The last point I want to make comes by way of one of my favorite biblical stories in the prophetic Book of Jeremiah. The young prophet is directed by God to purchase a piece of property and put the deed in a clay jar, and bury it. This he did. Simple enough. Yet the property was in a war zone. The Babylonian army was about to lay siege on all of Juda along with the young prophet's purchase. What Jeremiah was told to do would be the equivalent of me purchasing land in Aleppo, a once populous city in Syria that was decimated by a four-year bombing campaign by the Syrian dictator, Bashar Assad. Yet, the biblical story points to hope. Despite the oncoming invasion of the land the prophet just purchased, it was a sign of hope. Jeremiah's God would have the last word in Jeremiah's day. I believe that same God will have His "word" to stand in this day as well.

"ZOOM-X" by David Zuber

It was just a short announcement at the end of a newscast. Something that I thought was just a filler. A new virus had been discovered in a city in China, Wuhan,… a place I had never heard of, in the middle of the country. How many times had we heard something like this before – a plague was emerging? I remembered the furors over Ebola, Zika, SARS, etc. They had never turned into worldwide medical emergencies, so I quickly dismissed this corona (was someone getting even with the manufacturer of my favorite imported beer?) virus as 'fake-news" or at least exaggerated news. Nevertheless, it did not go away! Wuhan was locked down. Extreme measures were taken to keep people socially isolated. Drones were used to monitor who was on the streets. I was amused by the news clip of an old woman walking along the street. A drone swooped down and a voice emanating from the drone ordered, "Grandma, you must go home now!" The startled woman twirled around but no one was nearby. Then she looked skyward and the eerie voice repeated the same message. She turned and retraced her steps home. Our President bellowed "Nothing like this could happen in America" a bemusing assurance. I had discontinued believing anything he said, but I definitely wanted to believe him on this. If you want to believe something, you forget who is giving you the message. As the numbers of the infected and dead continued to rise exponentially, the White House assured us this was a Chinese disease (Kung flu). It was a result of the diet or the hygiene or the genes there. It would not come to America because we were no longer going to allow flights from

China to deplane in the US. Later we learned to our anger, but no surprise, that tens of thousands of people would later arrive from China.

One day the news shifted from China to northern Italy where an outbreak was reported of the corona virus (renamed Covid-19). What possible connection could there be between northern Italy and Wuhan, China? It no longer was a disease limited to a region of China. Weeks later, I read that Chinese laborers who worked in the manufacturing and agricultural sectors in northern Italy had carried the virus back with them from China after returning home to celebrate the New Year – the "Year of the Rat."

By early March, the virus had launched a two-prong attack on the United State. New York City in the east and Los Angeles and Seattle in the west were the first "hotspots" to emerge.

The Governor of California enacted a stay at home order. Fear of the virus kept me home. The first few weeks I was stayed in total isolation. Surprisingly to me, I adapted easily. I had a routine that I soon followed religiously. Breakfast around seven followed by watching the national news until eight and then a long walk with my dog. We walked along the river below my house. It was remote and it was a rare moment to meet another walker. We enjoyed the river and forest immensely. It was calming, reassuring, and a great way to start the day. Returning home, I would spend some time reading and then it was time for lunch. Afternoons were filled with housework (my house had never been so clean), yard work or attending Zoom meetings. I was a member of a local club and on the board of a local charity. Both decided to hold meetings via Zoom. Evenings consisted of watching shows on Netflix or Amazon Prime. I soon discovered the pleasure of reuniting via the Internet or phone with old friends. I made it a daily habit of conferring with an old friend. The value of friendships was immeasurable during the first few months of the pandemic. Some friends I would speak to several times a week; others would be monthly but we all shared the need to connect with others. Most of our conversations ended with "I love you;" something new and reassuring for me.

Zoom was my way of connecting with friends along with attending board and club meetings. In early April, I attended a Zoom board meeting. I sat on the board of a local non-profit that concerned itself with the welfare of senior citizens in my community. Most counties in the United States have similar agencies.

Being in a rural county it was often beneficial to connect with other rural counties to discuss common issues, obstacles and concerns. Zoom is a video-conferencing program that allows a group of people from various geographical regions to meet via the Internet. It has become wildly popular since the arrival of Covid-19 and the subsequent stay at home advisories. The host invites attendees to the meeting. At the scheduled time, attendees connect with the host via the Internet. Attendees have the option of attending with audio only or video and audio. If video and audio are chosen, you attend the meeting and everyone else can see and hear you. If audio only is chosen, only your voice is shared with other attendees. Others only see a box with your name or a profile photo projected on it. Choosing the audio only option allows a person to attend without worrying about appearance. An attendee could be stark naked and no one else would know.

At first Zoom seemed a Godsend. I could "zoom" with friends; attend club or board meetings; even interview job applicants. Zoom took over my calendar and a new verb entered my vocabulary. I "zoomed" or texted with my friends daily. I spoke to an old friend in Senegal, friends in England and relatives in Switzerland. Zoom was a wonderful way to connect with old friends and break the boredom of isolating at home.

I also discovered I could attend Zoom meetings sponsored by universities and other educational institutions. One day a friend, Spencer, and I decided to attend a virtual meeting concerned with the issue of civil rights in our country with a special emphasis on the senior population. There were to be several consecutive meetings on the topic and participant input would be encouraged.

I signed into the Zoom meeting from my computer about the same time that Spencer did from his home. The moderators were professors specializing in race relations, conflict management and geriatrics. Before we entered the meeting, we were asked not to join with our video on. We should enter with only audio and our first names on the screen.

Professors Kelly and Taylor welcomed us and explained that to create a safe environment for honesty and sharing they had decided video would not be permitted and only first names or aliases would be used. If we desired, we could also use a speech distorter to mask our voices and accents. It was further explained that there would be some simple ground rules that we would need to adhere to during the session. These rules were very simple: only one person could speak at a time, no use of derogatory epithets directed at another participant and that confidentiality of what was discussed within the meeting would be maintained. If a participant did not follow these guides one of the moderators would "mute" the offender and, if necessary, bar him/her from future meetings. By this time, I noticed a few people had left the meeting. Those remaining were asked to verbally agree to the ground rules. Each person verbally agreed and I discovered we had a group of around 45 people in attendance. The rules had certainly set the foundation for a "safe" meeting place but not being able to see and visually connect with the others was disconcerting. I realized that what I would share with one person might not be necessarily be received in the manner intended. So much depended on visual factors: sex, race, age, appearance of the "other". Taking those markers away could encourage openness and honest communication but could also make one reticent to share. Without the visuals, our biases might not easily show.

Our leaders shared with us their backgrounds and then asked participants to introduce themselves. We shared names and our profession prior to retirement but not much more. My ears were alert to any hint of a regional dialect or immigrant accent. Was that the clipped English of a Native American, the rolling r's of a South African, the molasses slow speech of a Southerner, the standard American dialect of California, the "r" pronounced as an "a" of the New Yorker, the slang of Ebonics, the romantic French accent or the harsh German? I tried so hard to listen for subtle speech differences that everyone sounded the same. Were they all middle class, white senior citizens? One voice did catch my attention. It was the timbre and quality. It was a voice that I could not identify as male or female, a rich, husky, delicate, sexy voice—a voice of kindness, empathy, strength and occasional vulnerability. A voice that intrigued me, a voice that I would not soon forget, a voice that resonated in my mind for several minutes. I was so mesmerized by the voice that I did not hear what was actually said by the speaker.

The participants had a variety of professional backgrounds. Several had been educators, with a smattering of attorneys, sales people, a bartender, a correctional officer, dancer, a gambler, and a truck driver among others.

Our moderators explained that we would be discussing current events with an historical perspective provided by them. We would discuss the issue in a broad context but would then need to personalize the issue by sharing incidents from our lives. We would also have reading and other assignments to complete between zoom classes. This did not thrill me but my alternatives were sorely limited during this pandemic.

Our first assignment was to work with another student to share incidents in our lives where we felt out of place and uncomfortable. We would be assigned partners via a random drawing conducted by our professors. Spencer and John were assigned to each other. I was assigned to Chris. We were asked to zoom text our partners to set up a virtual meeting time to discuss the assignment. With the pandemic raging, most people had lots of spare time to kill. We decided to meet via Zoom mid-morning of the next day. I had not spoken with or seen Chris but looked forward to meeting someone new. The boredom of a single life in rural America had been compounded by the raging pandemic; a new person in my life was welcome.

After a fit-full night's sleep, I awoke early, had breakfast and then took my dog for a long walk through a nearby park. I was curious and anxious about meeting Chris. After a long shower I dressed in one of my best shirts, made sure my hair was well groomed (this was a challenge since my barber's shop had been closed for two months) and even spritzed myself with Chanel for Men before remembering this was a virtual meeting. One last thing—empty my bladder before the meeting - men at my age often have uncontrollable urges – then I was ready but still endured a tortuous 10 minutes of waiting before Chris entered the Zoom waiting room.

For a second, I debated whether to enter the waiting room with my audio and visual connections on. I decided to have my audio turned on. It was a good decision because Chris entered the room only with audio on. Chris greeted me with a "Hi Dave" and I was astounded to hear the deep, raspy, sexy voice from the prior day. What a stroke of luck! Fantasies were running through my mind when I replied with a rather weak and timid "Hi Chris. Shall we turn our cameras on?" "I'd rather not. I think our assignment would best be done without any visuals. I think it might take away from our ability to share honestly." That brought me back to earth, but it did make sense. "That's fine with me."

There were some awkward moments as we began to get to know each other, but by the end of our 30 minutes I discovered that both Chris and I:
Liked gardening, hiking, dogs, empty beaches, tropical rainstorms, ice cream, art museums, our families, Thai food, being retired and Don Lemon.
We did not like Trump, high school, our first kiss, Algebra, The Simpsons and fast food.
At the end of the conversation, we decided to continue talking the next day since we had not even attempted to do the class assignment.

After signing off, I was so taken by Chris and the conversation I took another long walk with my dog. I could not get Chris out of my mind. So many images of what Chris might look like raced through my mind. I could not settle on one so just let my imagine run wild hoping the images would stop. That did not happen. I tried to watch TV but could not concentrate. Ditto with reading the newspaper. This unease mingled with desire had to be a result of self-isolating for so many weeks. Fantasizing must be connected with lack of interaction with other people. On the other hand, could I be coming down with

COVID? Was having delusional thoughts a symptom? In addition, a fever and cough? Well, not cough but let me check my temperature… no fever. The best remedy for this would be to smoke some good Humboldt weed.

Our second meeting was much like the first. We continued to learn more and more about each other. Our cameras remained off and neither one of us questioned that. I could not believe how much we had in common. Chris had great jokes and comebacks to my remarks. We talked about our love of music and the arts. She had taken violin lessons as a child and I had taken piano. I had taken an Art history class in college from a dynamic professor who had shared his passion for art with his students. It had turned out to be one of my favorite classes. Chris had the same experience with a similar course at her university.

Our second meeting ended with Chris asking if I liked to play games. This piqued my curiosity and I rather quickly replied "Sure". "Well, I have a game that we might enjoy. I will show you tomorrow. Just think of some of your favorite pieces of western art."
"Sounds good".

Naturally, my fantasy-centered imagination went into overdrive with the thought of an "internet" art game. Would we assume the poses of famous pieces of art? Perhaps Chris would pose as one of Ruben's voluptuous women. Obviously, the stay at home order was heightening my senses and sparking my imagination. Even my body reacted in ways that I had not experienced in years (now use your imagination!).

Chris explained the game at our next Zoom meeting: jigsaw on-line. From the site's gallery of artworks one of us would select an art piece, which was then disassembled into jigsaw puzzle pieces. Each player took turns selecting a piece to see where it fit in the puzzle.   The first one to guess either the name of the piece or the artist would win the round.   Since I had not taken an Art History course in 50 years this was going to be a challenge.

Chris selected her artwork and had it disassembled into jigsaw pieces and presented them to me. She had made it easy.   I only had ten pieces of fit together to complete the piece.   I constructed the puzzle -- Michelangelo's Creation of Adam. We had both seen it in the Sistine Chapel and been overwhelmed with its beauty and majesty. A few years ago, I had even contemplated having a portion of it tattooed on my back.

The next day I presented Chris with a puzzle of Henri Matisse's Blue Nude. She guessed it correctly. Over the course of the next few weeks, our puzzles covered Bosch's Garden of Earthly Delights, Goya's Nude Maja, Modigliani's Reclining Nude, etc.   We joked that we had narrowed our topic to nudes but our daily conversations covered so many different things.   I felt safe sharing my thoughts, dreams, and fears with Chris and she did with me. We had created an amazing relationship.   I dare not miss one of our daily meetings.   They had become the highlight of my life in quarantine.

One day Chris presented me with a puzzle that when put together would be a photograph taken by a well-known photographer. I was able to name the photographer, Robert Mapplethorpe, but did not recall the title of the piece. It was entitled "Embrace". I marveled at the beauty of the entwined bodies. It was a haunting photo of two nudes (one white and one black) cradling each other. Although the viewer cannot tell the sex of the couple, it was a very erotic piece of art.

In a short time, chats with Chris had become an essential part of each day. She was a confidant, counselor, confessor and fantasy all wrapped up in one person. We communicated using audio. However, we never discussed switching on the video to see each other.

My old friend Spencer texted me one day to see what I was up to. He had not seen me in the Zoom class (that had gone by the wayside since the conversations and games with Chris were my priority). He asked about my partner and I told him how much we enjoyed each other's company and how attracted I was to her.

TEXT TALK #1

Spencer: So you really like this Chris, huh?

Me: She's really cool and we just click. ♡

Spencer: That deep voice with a weird accent?

Me: Accent?

Spencer: Not standard American English. What's her real name?

Me: Chris!

Spencer: Have you swapped photos?

Me: No.

Spencer: No last name, no photo, weird accent.   She asked you for $ yet?

Me: FU 👆

Spencer: Maybe her real name is

Christina😺   or

Kristen or

Chrisoluru

Krishna   👳

Me: FU in the ASS!

End of conversation.

It really didn't matter to me where Chris was from; she was a special person to me.   My fantasies about her features were not always the same.   One day she'd be Asian, another day African, another time European.   She was changeable   physically   but   always   had   the   same psychological, moral and ethical qualities that I loved.

One day Chris's puzzle was Basquiat's "Irony of the Negro Policemen".   This was the day after George Floyd's memorial service in Chicago and she'd chosen this piece to commemorate the day.   We'd both watched the service on television.   We were both touched by the eloquence of the speakers,   especially   Al   Sharpton.   The   Black   Lives Movement encouraged demonstrations.   Even in my small town,   a   group   gathered   weekly   to   demand   changes. Confederate statutes were removed, place names changed, racist sport mascots replaced.   It was an uplifting time in the midst of a pandemic and a dearth of competent federal leadership. Living in a MAGA County with few fellow progressives it was a relief to converse with a like-minded person. What a blessing to have someone like Chris in my life during these troubling times.

One day as we were talking via Zoom Chris, hit me with a question "Have you ever wondered what I look like?" Trying to act nonchalant I responded "Well, yes but you never wanted to see me before, right?"

"Well I guess it would be like show me yours and I'll show you mine --- photo I mean", Chris' response ended with her hearty laugh.

"OK, but you know I'm nearly 70 so don't expect a Brad Pitt".

"That's fine but I'm nearly your age so let's do it."

"I'm not sure I want to do it all at once, like live. How about if we share photos?"

"Sounds good to me. I have an idea I will share with you. Have a photo handy when we talk tomorrow."

It must have taken me hours to decide on the right photo. I wanted it to be honest so I eliminated any photos taken more than 2 years earlier. No photo shopping.   I eliminated any photos with other people in them.   Then I had to decide if it would just be a face shot or full body.   Ended up with full bod; fully clothed.

The next day I was waiting for Chris when she entered our Zoom space. After our usual chitchat, she asked if I had a photo nearby.   I had.   "Don't be disappointed but it's fully clothed, fully frontal".

"That's cool; mine's the same".

"Great" I responded trying not to sound too excited. On the other hand, was I anxious? Did I really want to see Chris? I had had so many fantasies and I enjoyed that. After seeing her photo, I would only have one.

"So here's the deal. We will scan our photos into this puzzle program. Then we can divide our photos into pieces just as if we did with the masterpieces. We each get to pick one piece a day and then our photos will slowly emerge. Sound like a plan?"

"OK, that's cool. But it'll be weeks before we construct the full puzzle/photo".

"That's right. With this pandemic, all we have is time. We're going to be cooped up for a long time to come."

"Yeah I guess you're right"

We scanned our photos and turned them into dozens of puzzle pieces. We would each send the other one piece each day. After our conversation for the day, we would place the piece in its correct place on the puzzle grid. Each day I would send her a randomly chosen puzzle piece. I would receive one from Chris in return.

It actually was fun. After about a week, I realized that it was going to take quite a while to put this photo puzzle together. One piece was a big toe. Another piece was an ear lobe and others that consisted of several of pieces of the same fabric that she was wearing. I was a little disappointed. I was even more intrigued when I realized her photo was in black and white.

TEXT TALK #2

Spencer: Wassup?

Me: Not much. U?

Spencer: Just chillin''. Almost done with the class that you bailed on.

Me: 😄

Spencer: How's Chris? Picture?

Me: Fine. Talk every day. No pic

Spencer: U crazy

Me: She's cool – 💕

Spencer: 😖. Fantasy does not = reality. That voice is weird.

Me: Sexy

Spencer: Masculine. Chris can be a man's name.

Me: FU

Spencer: U obsessed.

Me: Gotta go

I was angry with Spencer and myself. He was right in some ways. Since this pandemic, I was losing my sense of reality. Everything had changed. Normal activities like shopping or going to a restaurant had become fraught with danger. Dating in person was out. It was strange that Chris did not want to share pictures. It is cool to want to get to know someone before seeing him or her, but is it the new normal? It cannot be denied that physical appearance makes a difference in our society and in our lives. We reject this notion but it lingers in our subconscious, in our every assessment of another person. In a society of the blind, perhaps, physical characteristics would not be important.

Am I deceiving myself when I think I can love Chris unconditionally without regard to sex, race, or being physically challenged? Without a physical representation? Am I afraid of what that representation might be? Would it be a turn-off? Would my true reaction be a mockery of my self-image? Would it be a reflection of my deep-seated prejudices?

I was jolted out of my thoughts when a news bulletin flashed across the television screen. Demonstrations against systemic racism were taking place throughout the country. People were marching in large cities and small towns carrying placards "Black Lives Matter", "I Can't Breathe", "Say My Name!" Crowds composed of all ages, races and backgrounds were demanding change in our country. Demands that have been made, yet remain unfulfilled, since the birth of our nation. Righteous, noble demands, worthy demands that need to be embraced and made real.

My computer screen flashed; my computer was going into pause mode. I hit a key that brought my computer back to life, the pieces of Chris still to be placed into the puzzle. I glanced at the television screen. The juxtaposition of the two screens unnerved me. Was the dilemma I was facing not unlike the dilemma my society was facing? Are we brave enough, adult enough to put the pieces together to face reality or is it easier to be coddled in a fantasy of our own making?

Second Coming
"Heaven Sent"
by Diane Wilson Onwuchekwa

On Sunday a little girl sitting beside me at chapel, gave me her stuffed and sealed offering envelope. She filled out the offering envelope the best she could, her name, amount and zip code. From her handwriting, I believe she was 4 or 5 years old. The offering envelope was stuffed with something. I thanked her, shook her hand and held the stuffed seal enveloped.

I held the offering envelope for a while. The little girl asked me to open it, inside was the chapel bulletin folded, I looked at her name on the envelope, and her writing was not that legible, I think her name was "HEAVEN". I asked her mom if her name was "HEAVEN". Her mom said, "Yes."

This particular Sunday, I did come alone to this chapel service. Several months ago, my adult niece and her daughter moved in with me. That Saturday night my 10-year-old grandniece had a sleepover with three girls, ages 7, 10 and 11. Sunday morning, I was ironing my blouse and the seven-year-old girl asked where I was going, I said to church. She asked if she could go, I said, "Get dressed." All the girls wanted to go, so they all got dressed.

We arrived a little late but four little girls went to chapel on Sunday with my niece and me. When we arrived at the chapel, I had to park in the back because all spaces were taken up front. There was a pack of ice and snow when I got out of the car; I tried to avoid slipping, while I trying not to fall, immediately the 7 year old reached her hand to help me. She held my hand until I got in the chapel door.

I looked at the offering enveloped again that the little girl had given me. She had written her entire name on the offering envelope. "HEAVEN SENT HILL". I asked her mom is her name "HEAVEN SENT HILL." HEAVEN's mom told me that she gave birth to HEAVEN at 43 years old and that her daughter was HEAVEN SENT.

One of pages in the chapel bulletin had the words to the song "GLORY HALLELUJAH. The ten-year-old girl told me that she likes singing at the chapel and when we are going to sing "Glory Hallelujah". I told her because we came a little late, the song was already sung. In addition, she asked about Sunday school.

During chapel service, beautiful young women all dressed in white from Alpha Kappa Alpha Sorority made an announcement about community service activities they are sponsoring. The ten-year-old girl leans and tells my niece that she wants to join Alpha Kappa Alpha when she goes to college.

After the chapel service, the 7 year old said this is the second time that she has been to church in her life, and 10 year said this is her fifth time going to church. All girls told us that they really like this church.

Several months ago, my cousin told me that our home church in Virginia might close because they are down to ten regular members each Sunday.

That experience on Sunday, brought my attention that it is important for us to take children to church. I know several single women going to church every Sunday alone, praying for a husband and family. Just think, if 10 percent of all the single women in the church brought a child to church, I believe that 20 years from now churches will not be forced to close because of the lack of membership.

Now, we cannot go to church because of a pandemic.

Here is an offering you can give to the church and the body of Christ that can last through generations' unseen-- bring a child from your home or neighbor's home once the churches are safe to attend after the   pandemic.

Let us bring children to church! This is HEAVEN SENT.

"A Call of Freedom by Hamza Chafki

"I think, I didn't have to take all this" Chafik thought, feeling a sense of self- reproaching. It has been one month now that he spends sleepless nights and when it happens that he sleeps, they are nightmares about his prophecies of the new decision he has taken. Well, damn it! What kind of a life is it if we do not take risks? It is all about risks, is it! He who fears taking risks is the biggest coward and I do not want to be a coward... a lot of perplexing ideas echo in his mind as he thinks of his coming adventure. Chafik counts the days left for him to leave Morocco towards the USA, as a scholar of his culture and an ambassador of his language, Arabic. He sacrificed his new job as high school teacher and decided to live the American dream. 'It's New York, baby!' this always echoes in his mind whenever he googles NYC landmarks.

The day has come and the-last-minute fellow gathered few clothes, mostly traditional ones, a tajin, slippers and some herbs for tea to bewitch the American chicks once he gets there and make some new friends. "Dad, let's go it's time" He headed towards the door leaving the house where his family is crowded and tears in their eyes. It had always felt so strange to hug his family members, but it did not now, he gave each of them a tight hug with watery eyes and a tight throat unable to utter a word. "We will keep in touch, guys! Just don't forget to install Skype" He finally said with a shaky voice and turned his back to his family heading towards an unknown destination. "Be a man and look after yourself" His dad said and kissed him on both cheeks with a smile. "I will dad, thanks!" He replied and climbed the bus stairs towards his seat. Before sitting, he stole some last glances at his father from the bus window and did not want him to disappear from his eyesight, tears of happiness and sorrow coming down his eyes under the sunglasses that he put on as his shield to hide his weak feelings.

It was a long flight from Morocco to Germany and then to Los Angeles. 'Let's discover the world, and everything else can wait' He thought. Once in LAX airport, where many worldly known actors, singers have landed, Chafik walked down the hallway struck by the luxury and novelty of the place as well as the people. He followed the signs and hurried to catch his next flight to New York. "Who has ever thought that I would experience this "He thought to himself. The journey towards White Plains, Westchester in New York was delayed for one hour. Chafik felt so perplexed; his arrival would be an hour ahead and no doubts he would miss the person in charge of picking him up from the airport... What if he is gone by now, damn it! I do not even have enough money to get there... He dismissed all these negative ideas and decided to enjoy

The flight, instead. The blue color of the Pacific Ocean shines as the waves hug the sky while the plane took off from LAX airport; Chafik had been deeply immersed in his imagination of the newly coming experience and enjoying the American soil!

Once the plane landed in White Plains, the weather was so gloomy and the sky darkened. Chafik took his luggage and

headed towards the exit aimlessly in a rush. A strongly built bold person approached him doubted holding a white paper with a big bold name that reads "CHAFIK". Both a sense of relief and happiness overthrew Chafik's heart and looked at the man excitedly. 'Sir, are you Chafik?" The man asked politely, "uh_Hello, yes, sir I am" Chafik replied uncertainly. The person took both bags in one hand put them in the tank of the car and opened the door for him, "dog-gone man! Kidding me bruh, he is treating me like a king" Chafik thought and thanked the car driver, while climbing the brand-new Hyundai. "So, where did you come from?" The driver asked. "I came all the way from Morocco as a scholar here in Mercy College." Chafik replied. The man nodded his head admiringly saying, "Oh, hello brother, I am from Kenya. We are both Africans" "Yes, indeed" Chafik replied with a sense of merriment that came with the word 'Africans'. "You get me bruh ; Africa is a great land, but, alas, we have unwise greedy rulers" The driver told Chafik who was dreamingly enjoying the landscapes of Westchester county and enjoying the cozy seat as well as the heavy rain splashing on the car window, " Yeah bruh" Chafik said imitating the way Americans utter the word...
To be continued...

Second Coming
"A Corona Journey" by Askhat Aubakirov

I never actually realized the seriousness and dangers of this pandemic until now. During that time, I was studying in another country and observing how my plans were disintegrated as my visa expired. With all of this occurring, I made plans to return home to Kazakhstan through Moscow. However, my flight and agenda were abruptly interrupted due to coronavirus and I needed to find a feasible solution expeditiously. Therefore, I obtained a new flight plan, traveling to Kaunas, Milan, Istanbul, and Astana. Well, this was about to become an arduous task or should I just accept it as a tough journey with lots of uncertainties. To be sure, uncertainties are, indeed, hilarious to say the least!

Anyway, I boarded the plane from Kaunas, Lithuania, and began the journey. Bye, my comfort zone! The flight was brief, however, scenic, for this was the first time I saw Alpine Mountains from an aerial view and not from "Google Pics." What a joy!

The aircraft landed at Milan airport as this was the longest layover between flights I have ever experienced. It was more than 3 hours and exhausting. Now to my surprise, it was announced that a cancellation was occurring with 23 hours to wait until the next carrier to Istanbul! To make matters worse, I am a student; alone with only some milk money left and eager to go gallivanting in the to visit the Milan Cathedral, where one of my favorite opera singers, Andrea Bocelli, had a great live stream recently singing,

"Songs for Hope." Unfortunately, a man in security in the passport control section indicated that I could not leave the facility as my visa had already expired. Now, being anxious in a cultural city like Milan and confined to an International Airport was trying. I about to lose my mind. I had absolutely anything to do and no one really wanted to talk to me. No offense, but it seems like Italians are not big fans of English, huh? Yeah, I get it - why should a Rome Empire descendants care too much about speaking this, English thing? Anyway, I began searching for additional tourist information in Milan.

I came up with an exciting idea. I found the VR mode of observing the city in Google Maps and started wandering near the Cathedral virtually. Well, I have to say, with the available technology and the imagination; I was there, inasmuch as I was stuck in the airport. Okay, let us be honest, I was just trying to convince myself that everything was okay. It was for the moment and the moment was all needed. Maybe, one day I will be lucky enough to forget the details and truly believe I was there physically.

These 23 hours were of waiting were absolutely torture. After all, prior to the pandemic, everything was at my fingertip. For the first time, I was introduced to loneliness-my phone was about to die; no one was online to talk to me; a global time difference; and my imagination was at its best.

Therefore, I had a very good time there thinking about everything I could. For example, I was thinking about what exactly I should have said debating with some person a few years ago. Oh, my life would be so much better now!

Suddenly, I get the news that a new pandemic wave was already in Kazakhstan. Therefore, quarantine is imposed in the country. A few minutes later, I received additional pressing news that Turkey closed its borders to Kazakhstan and all the flights were canceled. Whoa! I was lucky again! Now, I prepared for being confined in Istanbul for some time! Yeah, unexpected stressed-out journey! I tried to talk to airlines and the only solution they had was waiting for the government to make a move.

I have to admit the fact this pandemic taught me how to expect the best but be prepared for the worst. I soon landed in Istanbul. However, I cannot connect to Wi-Fi. Oh man, not this! How can a "zoomer" spend even a few minutes without Wi-Fi? Therefore, I went to the Istanbul Airport information desk regarding the Wi-Fi. I was told, "If you wish to connect to the free Turkish Wi-Fi, you need to buy a not-free Turkish sim-card, which costs 30 euros".

I heard a lot about the Turkish service, but now I witnessed this s myself and it does not matter if you ever need the service, it always needs you anyway. I spent my last money to buy this sim-card and, of course, no longer needed the free Wi-Fi.

I had to spend three days in Istanbul, a big, loud, crazy city with twenty million people living in it. I moved to the cheapest hostel in the city center. It felt like Istanbul was the biggest representation of Disney Aladdin's vibes. Everyone was running somewhere. Everyone was selling something. Everyone was shouting out the prices, colors everywhere were extremely bright and over saturated.

I planned to go outside and take a walk in the evening. I left the hostel and suddenly heard shouting and gunshots. No way! It could not be true. A few minutes later, an ambulance and police with guns arrived. Therefore, I knew something was serious. Therefore, I decided not to leave the facility.

The next day I visited the Hagia Sophia right before the latest reformations of it into the mosque. Well, it was here that I said, "Perfect timing, finally".

One day in the cafe, I sipped a delicious cup of Turkish tea and I decided to thank the owner personally. Kazakh and Turkish are quite similar to each other, so I decided to say "rahmet", which means "thank you" in Kazakh. Shortly afterward, the owner was silent and appeared to be stunned because of the usage of the word, "rahmet." In Turkish the word means, "mercy" and is usually used to wish a person God's mercy and death with no suffering. Well, yeah, I was unaware that I had wished the owner to die peacefully. I am a good tourist and that was not my intention.

Once again, I had to change the flights due to cancellations. This time I needed to travel from Istanbul to Almaty and on to Astana, after that to Petropavlovsk to my final destination- home.

It was a tough journey. Eventually, I came back. According to the extremely big amount of tired people in the airport, I can suggest I was not the only one experiencing such. Moreover, if I had to do it again, I would! "Home... How sweet the sound!"

"Can-SURVIVE" by   Felicia A. Andrews Bryant

Throughout most of our lives we have been told in one way or another to "fear not!" It is a basic command in some religious veins, but; we have all heard it expressed most deliberately through the historical memoirs of the late President F. D. Roosevelt. He pointed out most emphatically, "we had nothing to fear but fear itself!"

I had not fully realized how appropriate that statement was. Then at age 40, I saw the face of fear in my own face as my doctor reluctantly, but; as always, compassionately told me, "YOU have breast Cancer". At that precise moment it mattered not how diligent I had always been about "checkups" and mammograms. It did not matter that by having five children, I had also established a regular routine of doctor visits since the age of 20 years old. Who knew that 20 years into my personal future all that would matter is that word CANCER? I didn't even care where IT was. It only mattered that IT was.

My mind was racing in and out of an uncharted sense of me. I heard all of what Dr. Stang was saying: "early stages, radical mastectomy, chemotherapy. "
I then regained enough lucidity to ask my doctor, who was also a trusted friend, "What would you suggest I do?" His exact answer, "If you were, my wife, my sister, my daughter, I would advise you to have the radical mastectomy and the chemotherapy."
My first focus was consumed only with ME and visions of MY OWN mortality slipping away. Then, somehow those

thoughts were quickly dispelled by thoughts of my own husband and our children.

At that moment a quieter sense of sanity enveloped my thoughts. I quickly responded to the doctor by giving my consent to accept his plan.

Still thinking I had wiggle room, I asked if I might wait until June after school would be out and my crisis would be more convenient for all involved. My query was met with a resounding yet gentle "no!" The doctor continued by saying time is important but he could give me a week. I thanked him and my trust in him and my God now allowed me to move forward. I was content that this one week would be all I needed to encourage my children to understand what was happening to me and be encouragingly caressed by my husband who stood by me constantly.

Not yet ready to turn the lives of my husband and children over to a life without me, I asked myself what is best for my husband and our children? The answer... I am best for them. Fear would not rob me of the person I always wanted to be, a wife and mother. The elimination of fear in most any situation frees one's ability to fight. I had been armed with more information about MY personal insight.

I had begun to fight against the word "cancer" that had invaded MY life and by so doing I had also begun my fight to continue MY Life with MY family.

Thankfully for me I derived a great deal of strength from five women who blessed my life.

My mother had died in 1988, which was two years before my diagnosis. She had succumbed several strokes. My other mother, Gladys, was a precious gift that came to me as my mother-in-love, (aka mother in law). She had always been Momma too and so did the blessings continue.

Lydia, is my mother's only sister. She is an infectious blessing of optimism who comes equipped with a constant display of a beautiful smile. She went through a bilateral mastectomy and never lost that smile.

Alene is my husband's aunt and his mother's oldest sister. She had colon surgery and lived one week short of turning being 100 years of age.

Thelma, my mother's best friend also added her expertise to my survival life book. She had the same surgery as Myself, and showed no ill effects. She continuously spurred me on and kept me in tears of joy with her glorious sense of humor. These are just a few of the warriors God sent to assist me on my journey. I've lost their physicality, but; my heart is forever filled with their irreplaceable essence, love and who of them.

I believe whatever you've done in life prepares one for what one must do. Making choices of quality is all important.

I am blessed to have made an excellent choice in my husband. He never wavered once in his display of love, devotion and support, before during or after my surgery. This fact alone was a major step in allaying my fears.

It is vital to know your own family's health history. This information comes not to frighten one but to also arm one when and if one must fight. Knowing cancer may exist in one's family's history does not mean it will exist in one's life.

Knowing can assist you in gaining better insight and strength as I have learned.

I often think retroactively to that initial day when the word CANCER loomed so much larger than my life. On that day, I was faced with a dynamic challenge.

I made up in my mind, which is where the fear originated; that, I must be well. It mattered not how the doctor felt, nor even that God had intervened. It took me to get me to the right place at the right time. Choice is mine!

I continue to pray. I remain vigilant to my doctor visits. I exercise even though I could do more. I watch what I consume.

All I do is not out of fear. It is out of care, love of self and just better life maintenance.

I have reevaluated this word CANCER. It no longer frightens me. It encourages me.

I now know better how to navigate within the scientifically proven medical methods that has assisted in my optimum recovery.

The new word that evolved from my experience is "CAN-SURVIVE!"

"Now What?" by Michael D.Marks, II

It is appalling as to what is being presented to us all over the news - watching our demise on camera by bigots and crooked police officers while the offenders get preferential treatment. Now, we go through the emotional cycle of sadness, shock, trauma, anger, and hopelessness. What is most frustrating and what anyone that opposes us can see coming is our response.

I do not have a problem with the looting because it is all those emotions bottled up in that particular area and too much fear to unleash them on who truly deserves it, as well as the genius of racism, for it has no face so people lash out. I never criticize people for that type of frustration because it is easy to be critical while typing on social media or observing people from the safety of our homes.

For years, I have emphasized that we are our own saviors. I have encouraged economic boycotts for more than seven years but our addictions to shopping and being followers of anything-popular keeps us controlled.

The pandemic showed us just what a month of not shopping could do to this economy. Imagine if we planned for this and did not do any extra shopping for two months while also devising a strategic action plan of supporting local elected officials financially and with our votes to win key political positions in our respective areas so that we can affect local legislation to carry out our agendas for equality.

Can you imagine grooming our young people in a manner of economics, self-awareness, black pride, and the ability to defend themselves early?

The Panthers taught us that defending ourselves against the police is necessary; especially while our people are constantly, being arrested with guns was effective. Dr. Martin Luther King, Jr. taught us that when our people are of one collective mindset, we are able to affect legislation. Imagine how effective the message would be if we as a people voted down ballot in presidential elections when no candidate meets our needs and demands?

We have this game all wrong. We have black people in this society who are thriving economically, socially, and politically. However, it is being done in a selfish manner because as soon as we thrive we want to "stunt" on the very people we claim to love instead of simply enjoying our success while reaching that hand back and uplifting those who demonstrate the will to succeed.

Black Wall Street is a reality that we can recreate only better with its own police force of mostly black and brown and more lawyers as well as judges that adequately represent our community. It is not that we disagree with policing. However, we do disagree with the "gang culture" of policing.

If we truly want to level the playing field, we have to level up culturally because racism is not going anywhere. Therefore, our response to it has to change. For those of who stand there and record your fellow man being shattered by the police, you are complicit in their demise. So, walk away if you are not going to help. I do not advocate having all of the solutions. However, I care enough to be a part of one that is grounded in sound logic, tangible goals, and with a focus on us always advancing within this society collectively.

Peace!

"The Sabotage of Digital Filter, Trophy Culture and Trauma Browsing Syndrome (TBS): Seeds of the Great Disconnect" by William Ashanti Hobbs,II

Recently, I presided over a department meeting where many of my faculty lamented the difficulties coercing students to pass out papers while they take roll or write classroom instructions on the board. "I don't know these people" seems to be the usual reason to object. One of many chosen students appears clueless even after it is explained that simply reading the names aloud from the paper handles the issue. As the faculty continued to talk, I discovered that all assignments requiring a deeper level of social interaction, like peer reviews and group projects, now draw more ire from students than ever before. This drives home the fact that educators now have students who are willing to take whatever penalty is issued for not reaching out to the student next to them in order to be caught up on whatever it is that they have missed due to absence. In short, we now have a generation of college students (in some cases, even those who are high-performing) willing to let their grades, among other aspects of student life, suffer to avoid collaborating or interacting with one another.

Simply ranting about how these kids do not make sense is pointless. I decided instead to identify the causes of what I term The Great Disconnect. This term defines the cultural shift that has taken place over the past twenty years (2000–2020) where a digitized generation undergoes social distancing where asocial, introverted sensibilities are taken to a level that is self-sabotaging. This is a level where basic manners, collegiality, simple conversation are made to seem abnormal and cause irreversible harm to relationships, productivity and an overall sense of community.

Beyond trying to sound clever with newly coined phrases, I wanted to discover strategies to combat this disturbing trend. I began by reviewing, remembering, and recalling milestones in my two son's lives, going over pictures and videos of little league games, spelling bees, and birthday parties. The enduring awkwardness of social development throughout the stages of childhood was there as expected. As I looked closer, I sensed a lingering obstruction in that area that seemed to underscore, or I dare say menace, every frame. It was an obstruction that came from two causes, both at play in varying degrees, but with consistency nonetheless: digital filters and trophy culture.

Digital Filters

Kids ran around and sang songs at birthday parties of the past. Congratulations were given over cool presents received. An eager shake of the shoulder or pat on the back was given to the giver of the present. As I watched videos of my sons' more recent birthday parties, the number of kids fell to handfuls if that, most of which drifted off into corners with their cellphones or the living room's video game system. Kids got and grew to expect gift bags for even coming to the party at all. It was as if kids needed to be bribed to disengage enough from the safety of their own world of social media, video games and texting to be open to any social connection. In addition, these parties were not even during the standoffish, too-cool-to-make-an-effort-to-participate teen stage. No, this was a hindrance that made itself apparent as early as fifth grade.

Instead of legitimate interaction, we promise our babysitters that they will only have to provide pizza from the fridge and an occasional juice box as the kids babysit themselves with Netflix, endless YouTube and Vine videos. Cell phones are now accepted at dinner tables, the last place for everyone to check in with each other, that is if everyone else is even at the table at all. Laptops are now taking residence next to the dinner table's fruit bowl or floral arrangement. Hey, the kids do most of their schoolwork on the laptop. Who wants to interrupt that? Yes, I'm guilty as well. I started drafting this essay from a laptop at the dining room table, next to my eighth-grade son's laptop. No, he is not at the table working on an assignment. I have allowed him to slide into the habit of leaving it there instead of putting it back on the desk in his room, as if eating with one hand and watching God knows what on this laptop forever supersedes a basic conversation between us.

"Whatev," as the kids say. Yes, that is on me for facilitating, allowing, and the subversiveness.
Facing my culpability enables me to see how these digital natives (C.Halton, 2019) traveling that same path through high school, can wind up in my classrooms taught by digital immigrants like myself and be lacking fundamental steps of social development due to far too much time with technology or worse, getting poor imitations of those critical experiences through digital filters. Social media is a petri

dish of such poor imitations. People are emboldened to be far crueler and thoughtless behind the veil of screen names and avatars. A child can get his or her first understanding of a prolonged discussion from miserable people trolling discussions for attention. The most questionable TV show when I was coming up was Jerry Springer. This low-level talk show ended episodes of staged brawls, threats and chair-throwing to cheering crowds with some simple lesson or moral that the participants clearly were brought in and paid not to exemplify or demonstrate. These children have grown up on reality TV shows that go even further than Jerry Springer does. Their reality TV shows carry the sole purpose of giving the most fame and status to people who have the biggest meltdowns. Moreover, as if that is not enough, kids now bypass the context of the conflict by simply playing highlights of hair-pulling, table overturning and drinks thrown in people's faces. The effects show up around them when the behavior is mimicked in videos posted of their peers attacking each other in cafeterias and getting belligerent with teachers.

Presumably then, living behind digital filters could seem safe, since one watches from a screen, but with such a disturbing orientation as that to life "out there," how can a child not get the impression that quarantining themselves behind a screen for life is best? Aside from the present-day mandate that people stay at least six feet from each other in this strange time of contagion, how could a child not see that dealing with people face to face, on the fly with no pause button, is something to be avoided at all costs?

Holly Shakya, assistant professor in the division of global public health at the University of California, San Diego, asserts that there is conclusive evidence that "replacing your real-world relationships with social media use is detrimental to your well-being."(K. Hobson, 2017) And what of those who half-heartedly try to engage but, upon stumbling across the awkward moments of life, find the lure of escaping into a screen too irresistible? Therein lies the means in which so many formative year opportunities to pick up and learn social cues are lost due to distractions.

Approaching someone they have a crush on in school can end and die with an unresponded like on a post. Trying to negotiate a dispute between classmates through tone-deaf texts goes haywire when trust is betrayed through screenshot exchanges sent to third parties. Not every clumsy decision stays with trusted friends who could tease them now and again. Now, those decisions live forever on social media, taking on a life of their own at the most inopportune moments. Untrained in the simple art of introducing one's self, people troll their way into and sour exchanges for they know no other way to become part of healthy discussion. Consequently, dealing with the basic learning experiences the rest of us navigated through in order to learn empathy, resiliency, consideration and gain a broader perspective on group dynamics are seen as unnecessary trauma. You ask your child to accompany you to the hospital where their aunt is in the 19th hour of labor and needs family support. You assure your child that they can stay in the waiting room. Your child says, "that seems like a lot going on. I'll just stay here and watch Netflix." A dear friend of the family is having a rough time of things and you offer them to come and spend a few days at the house. Your child says, "Can't she just get a hotel? She always start talking to me even when I'm playing video games (which is clearly all the time)." One of your parents, and thusly, your child's grandparent, has died and now the funeral is scheduled. Your child: "I don't do funerals because it's just too depressing. I've already texted everybody how sad I am about Grandpa dying anyway."

A colleague of mine said she had a nightmare of having died and being cremated, against her wishes, and sent to her children in an urn via UPS, skipping any sort of memorial service in her honor. Why would she have that nightmare? Because she has coddled and sheltered her kids from dealing with any difficult situations by allowing them to hide behind the screens of IPhones, Nintendo switches, iMacs and PlayStations. Now, the way her kids see it, difficult but necessary events are just too unpleasant and inconvenient, too much to unpack and put in perspective.

Hiding behind digital filters then, would seem like an easy fix. Clearly though, life in the digital realm is not all smiley-faced emoticons and silly memes. Cyber-bullying could not be the phenomenon that it is if that were the case. Therefore, how does such a bereft kid, now in college, cope with all of the carnage and toxicity they witness through the digital filters of social media and technology? They cope with more of it, especially many on their way to college. After all, however toxic and draining technology, video games and social media are, they are still predictable, especially in a new world of a new campus with strangers, professors, and challenging workloads.

These disconnected students hole themselves up in their dorm rooms with video games and claim proudly to be introverts as if calling shotgun on a ride to the store. Beyond simple immaturity, they are more than likely to find themselves in disagreements with roommates presumably just as socially delayed and proudly inconsiderate as they are. The disagreements tend to astound others from having to revolve around the basic skills of communication, sharing and, teamwork — to a degree that seems more like second-graders in a sandbox figuring out the pecking order between one another than young adults learning the ropes of cohabitation.

The disconnected are much quicker to complain of being bored and homesick. As one would imagine, they are more apt to entertain the idea that college is not for them. They miss meeting with advisors, study groups, student organizations that serve as support systems. They bring that same energy into classrooms, refusing to put down their phones or take ear pods out of their ears. Professors calling on them to contribute to class discussions offend them. They insist on working alone when group assignments are required. They glare contemptuously when expected to speak when their name is read from the roll. In short, they miss the full potential of their success. This is not an attack on genuine introverts, this is an attack on a cultural shift that has made it either unpopular or downright suspicious for all students, introverts, ambiverts and extraverts alike, to tap into and develop interpersonal skills needed not only in university settings but also in the workplace and life in general.

Trophy Culture

The second cause of the Great Disconnect is the trophy culture and yes, I am certain I contributed to this, too. Congratulations and accolades are given now for merely showing up to a little league soccer game in the team uniform or a birthday party (yes, gift bags for a kid coming to a child's party is a pet peeve of mine). All attempts at encouraging them to step up their game to participate at their highest level can come under fire for being harsh and abusive, leaving parents and mentors and coaches to feign a blind eye to such shortcomings instead of addressing them.

Taken into the later years of co-captains and co-presidents of various teams and groups (as to not to offend anyone), a child with this background can question their identity and self-worth at the slightest disappointment, rejection or tough criticism. Not being chosen right off for a fraternity, sorority, scholarship, college or any other highly competitive prize or position means there is no point in trying a second time. Not doing well on an entry-level test for a highly competitive university automatically means considering alternatives as opposed to simply buckling down and giving more effort for a second try. A grade on a subject that has always come easy but has somehow fallen to a midterm C must be dropped with no questions asked. After all, they never had to work that hard before, for anything. Consequently, surely this is not the moment to rise to a higher level of difficulty in the subject as the rest of us had to at some point.

No, for this new generation, such a challenge is written off as a customer service issue, a stalling of ever-present grade inflation or if that fails, some sort of existential crisis. After all, no one they admire shows their crappy days of struggle and deep self-analysis on social media. The endless highlight reels of trophy-worthy posts make staying up to study, cutting back time to goof off with friends or facing their own toxicity and shortcomings unimaginable. Everybody is living his or her best lives. Major personal setbacks amplify all of the uneven comparisons to such manicured presentations. The risk of such awkwardness and vulnerability, to them, seems too great.

Therefore, in the face of having to deal with this challenge, something, they tend to reason, beyond them has failed. This gives way to trauma browsing, where one grabs for any unpleasant happening in the past as an excuse not do the integral inner work needed to face the necessary present-day challenges of life. Trophy culture insists that said student is entitled to an easy run of life leading into adulthood. The student, therefore, blames any past incident for having rendered them too broken to develop the character needed to accept full responsibility for their response or lack thereof (in this instance, to become resilient enough to deal with the misunderstandings and challenges that come with learning and developing social skills, collaboration and effective communication). Everything else that is equally unsexy falls into the same category.

The homework that is due, the newly-minted ex-girlfriend that remains as part of the class, the time management needed to handle a part-time job and classes... this sudden onslaught of adulting's expectations that they carry their own weight, is made out to be far too much to deal with. And why? Because somebody showed up late for their fifth-grade dance recital, got them the wrong pair of Jordans when they tried out for basketball or gave them the wrong iPhone as a sixteenth birthday gift. Someone has to pay for him or her not having life as easy as everyone followed on Instagram.

Of course, there is a subjective spectrum on what legitimately counts as trauma, let alone trauma having a notable impact. The issue is when kids come into class looking to excuse and pass anything off as trauma to excuse not trying to grow and further develop in any way. I've witnessed this in several instances where helicopter parents have come in with the student to discuss a difficult class only to have the student become quite talkative in an attempt to trauma browse, or blame any personal shortcomings they could on their parents to justify their sense of helplessness and hopelessness.

Many trauma browse to the very end of a semester. It is difficult to decide how much the typical manipulation under a more sophisticated guise or genuine neurosis is. Kids will come up with excuses. They will test you and try anything under the sun before having to "grow up." This is nothing new. Thank goodness for sound testing and diagnoses. It is a priceless safeguard in keeping the disconnected from thinking that the world will be responsible for tiptoeing around, in many cases, strategically placed triggers (especially the ones that are merely characteristics they simply refuse to improve upon).

Moving beyond such triggers takes more finesse than teaching only a decade ago. Now, when the culture of stunted social skills is coupled with the panic-stricken paralysis of facing any sort of hardship or challenge, the result goes beyond the tough love adage to grow up. This requires interventions concerning interpersonal skills, character-building talks; workshops on empathy, social navigation, soft skills, and many things we assumed came with "home training." Religion seems more taboo than ever. Either that or it is ripe for disregard due to patriarchy, racism and everything else that is wrong with the world. What is somehow thrown out along with religion is a space and emphasis for students to find the voice, the connection to something bigger than themselves to turn to beyond the self-medication of drugs and alcohol. A lack of spiritual base, in this day of hyper-diagnoses, can lead one down mistaken paths in order to evade the self-work needed to not only survive but also thrive in life. In short, the touchy subject of the importance of spirituality or one's faith should be addressed for further character development. This is especially the case with the health crisis that now menaces the world. Amy Sullivan, director of strategy for Vote Common Good, sees this moment as a great opportunity to reevaluate the power and use of faith:

"All faiths have dealt with the challenge of keeping faith alive under the adverse conditions of war or diaspora or persecution — but never all faiths at the same time. Religion in the time of quarantine will challenge conceptions of what it means to minister and to fellowship."(Politico, 2020)

Does this mean professors are now charged with raising their students along with educating them in a chosen subject? It does mean that we as educators may need to share moments of ourselves, our moments of finding inner strength and peace (most likely when we were their age) that would not make our Facebook highlight reel. We may need to relate a philosophical essay, short fiction piece or poem analyzed in class with the sudden death of one of our family members, when we didn't make the track team or a breakup we had in college (along with how we recovered from it).

I have come across a suggestion that seems to help bring the disconnected up to speed socially. It starts, as one would imagine, with students committing to blocks of time throughout the day where they are not dealing with any digital filters at all. This requires enough time for them to no longer fear silence, to embrace it and be acquainted with the sound of their inner voice. This is when they are most likely to sense that the constant white noise they swore they needed to think was actually a filter to keep them from deeper introspection. This is when they discover that their attention span is much greater than they imagined when not derailed by incessant pings of text and post notifications. During this time, they are to journal anything that they notice and learn about the world around them. I hope that they became adventurous and try this while out among others, quietly observing and documenting things they would have otherwise missed. The discoveries they find will reward them in a manner far richer than trinkets and euphemisms to pacify or normalize mediocrity.

Along with that, we as educators, parents and mentors need to share with these students' glimpses of our own curiosity with things we still have yet to comprehend. We may need to stop acting as though there was no sense of anxiety, uncertainty, and self-realization we had to wade through to get where we are. We may need to step beyond the lectern and check their self-absorption as they say, with love. In short, we may need to challenge ourselves about the way that we challenge them. It may be all that we have to build rapport and remedy the contagion of selfishness that detaches young people from the unpleasant work of accepting a greater sense of community. This acceptance would foster the responsibility needed to rethink reveling carelessly in packed bars, streets, and shorelines for Spring Break only miles away from the university office in which I finish this article. It would make them develop the empathy needed to consider family members and friends they could infect as unknowing carriers of the coronavirus.

The coronavirus pandemic has introduced to the masses the term social distancing. Quite honestly, the concept has been with us for quite some time due to the factors discussed and is a major component in what creates the Great Disconnect. We have more social distancing than we need thanks to digital filters numbing this generation's sense of compassion and understanding, along with the toxicity of social media.

Social distancing is doing just fine due to the trophy culture's infecting this generation with the idea that simply showing up to a situation or relationship with no dialogue, sense of compromise or contribution is acceptable. We can allow coronavirus prevention the concept of physical distancing us from endangering each other. Without encouraging badly needed social togetherness, our future will fall victim to a far more insidious pandemic.

"Eulogy- Ray Thomas" by Beryl A. Watson Shaw

"There are always two and only two trains running. There is life and there is death. Each of us rides them both." (A. Wilson, 1992).

I have drawn several parallels between August Wilson and Ray T. Whereas August Wilson, an African American playwright and author received two Pulitzer Prizes for Drama, Ray T's life experiences reflect and mirror the experiences of some of the characters that were created by Wilson.

The love that Ray T. Exuberated for his family and his Mother was unsurpassed. One of Wilson's Pulitzer Prize winning plays was titled *Ma Rainey's Black Bottom*. If there were a Pulitzer Prize for family love, Ray T. would have won it.

As a recipient of a Catholic education at St. Mary's School, Ray T. learned early in life that love is the most powerful weapon on earth and this weapon of love was the only weapon that Ray T. utilized in order to take him through his St. Croix Central High School experience, incident free.

Ray T. did not have to search far for role models. As a result, he was respectful and dignified as his Mother, Alice Turner Maynard, who held the awesome position as Deputy Clerk of the U.S. District Court on St. Croix. At her retirement banquet, judges and attorneys, including former Senate President Russell overwhelmed her with praises and accolades.

Ray T. was frugal and he managed his finances wisely. Perhaps, he had a spiritual and remote connection with Warren Buffet, but here at home, his sister Marcy

Jackson Encarnacion was an Administrative Secretary at Merrill Lynch for several decades.

Ray T. Resided in Sion Farm with his aunt Gaynel M. Turner during the latter part of his senior high school years. From that experience, he learned that everyone in that household went to school every day no matter if he or she were near death. He also learned that his aunt Gaynel ran the dietary department of the Juan Francisco Luis Hospital, without adequate compensation, for months when the Dietician Vera Falun was reassigned to St. Thomas.

Ray T. was employed at the Department of Education for several years. During those years, he forged a life-long and cherished relationship with Clinton Lang and the Lang Family. Ray T. also worked at the office of the Lieutenant Governor for several decades until his unforeseen disability in 2013.

August Wilson states that "to live life with dignity, to celebrate and accept responsibility for your presence in the world is all that can be asked of anyone." Wilson further states, "All you need in the world is love and laughter. That is all anybody needs. To have love in one hand and laughter in the other." (A. Wilson, 1982).

August Wilson died in 2005, at the age of 60.
Ray T. died in 2014 at the age of 55.

"Thoughts During the Pandemic and the Importance of
Religion in the African-American experience"
by James Arthur Holmes

For the past two centuries, Black Nationalism has been a
cyclical idea in the United States, fading away at times and
re-emerging with other forces at other times. Historically,
Nationalistic Movements among Blacks have fared best
when White resistance to Black progress has been most
intense. Black Nationalism has been most subdued when
there has been visible progress among Blacks. However,
when that progress is again impeded Black Nationalism
undergoes a resurgence (Bracey, Meier, Rudwick, 1970).

While several books and numerous articles have
examined Black Nationalism during the nineteenth century,
no major work has focused upon the relationship between
Black Nationalism and the theodicy question. Of the many
Black Nationalist figures, several were ordained ministers,
with three of the most prominent being Henry Highland
Garnet, Alexander Crummell, and Henry McNeal Turner.
While there are several biographies and books about these
persons and their nationalistic ideas, there are no works that
specifically focus upon the relationship between their
theodicies and their Black Nationalist positions.

Three researchers have provided the major speeches
and writings of Garnet, Crummell, and Turner: Earl Ofari,
*Let Your Motto Be Resistance: The Life and Thought of
Henry Highland Garnet*, Wilson Moses, *Destiny and Race:
Selected Writings/Alexander Crummell*, and Edwin Redkey,
*Respect Black: The Writings and Speeches of Henry
McNeal Turner*. These works form the fundamental
general sources for the study.

There are several specific collections for the study.
The archives of the AME Publishing House in Nashville,
Tennessee has copies of the *Christian Recorder*, the *Voice*

of Missions, and the *Voice of the People* that are gold mines about Turner information. The Special Collections Department of the Interdenominational Theological Center has a valuable Turner pamphlet, *Bishop Henry McNeal Turner Speaks to This Generation* (Atlanta: AME Church, 1982) by Josephus Coan. The New York Public Library has several original Garnet letters and various Garnet documents in the Schomburg Collection. The George W. Forbes Papers located in the Rare Book Department of the Boston Public Library offer various Crummell documents that reveal information on Crummell's early life. The Moorland-Spingarn Research Center at Howard University (Washington, DC) has the Henry McNeal Turner Papers.

Two previous Garnet researchers have focused mainly on his biography and his abolitionist thought and activities. *Sketch of the Life and Labors of Rev. Henry Highland Garnet* is basically a biography of Garnet's early life and says little about Garnet's theology, theodicy, or Black Nationalist position. (J. McCune Smith, 1891) In Earl Ofari, *Let Your Motto Be Resistance: The Life and Thought of Henry Highland Garnet*, there are two chapters, "Prophet of Revolutionary Black Nationalism" and "Racism, Religion, and the Black Struggle" that examine Garnet's Black Nationalist position and theology of resistance (E. Ofari, 1972). Ofari does not make the connection between Garnet's theodicy and his Black Nationalist position, however.

Joel Schor's *Henry Highland Garnet: A Voice of Black Radicalism in the Nineteenth Century* provides a thorough examination of Garnet's role in the Abolitionist Movement between 1840 and 1882 (J. Schor, 1977). Schor's research reveals three major Garnet contributions to the Abolitionist Movement. First, Garnet found the constitution to be an anti-slavery document for ideological purposes. Second, Garnet advocated civil disobedience and resistance on the part of slaves themselves. Third,

Garnet advocated a selective emigration to Africa and the glorification of the Black race that included self-pride and self-reliance. If Frederick Douglass is placed in the moderate camp among Black leaders advocating moral persuasions, legislation, and judicial decisions, then Garnet's role is brought clearer into focus, according to Schor. Schor's research reveals three major Garnet contributions to the Abolitionist Movement. First, Garnet found the constitution to be an anti-slavery document for ideological purposes. Second, Garnet advocated civil disobedience and resistance on the part of slaves themselves. Third, Garnet advocated a selective emigration to Africa and the glorification of the Black race that included self-pride and self-reliance. If Frederick Douglass is placed in the moderate camp among Black leaders advocating moral persuasions, legislation, and judicial decisions, then Garnet's role is brought clearer into focus, according to Schor. Schor's research is valuable for Garnet's Black Nationalist ideas and projects between 1840 and 1882. His research may be distinguished because he does not make the connection between Garnet's Black Nationalist position and his theodicy.

Crummell wrote an essay, "The Destined Superiority of the Negro" in which he delineated a belief that African-Americans were chosen by God for greatness. Crummell claims that slavery resulted from sins committed by prior African generations. Specifically, African foreparents refused to worship the true God, the God of Christianity. The knowledge of the true God, the Christian God, became less known from generation to generation, until the knowledge was completely lost. Crummell claims that God ultimately would liberate the slaves and restore them to supremacy: "the mighty seizes upon superior nations, and by mingled chastisement and blessings, gradually leads them to greatness" (Alexander Crummell, 1882).

Many studies focus on various aspects of the life and thought of Turner. However, we are without studies exclusively concerned with Turner's theodicy in relation to his Black Nationalist position. Mongo Ponton wrote a biography of Turner, *The Life and Times of Henry McNeal Turner* two years after his death, but the work is "slim and uncritical" and says nothing directly of Turner's theodicy and very little about his Black Nationalist position. (Stephen Angell, 1992)

Traditionally, there were four prominent periods of American Black Nationalism: (1) from 1790 to 1820; (2) the late 1840's and the 1850's; (3) the 1880's into the 1920's; and (4)since the early 1960's. (Bracey, Meier, Rudwick) Throughout American history, there has generally been varied approaches to Black racial problems. Some thinkers tended towards integration and assimilation, while others tended towards nationalist and separatist ideology. When the latter dominated the former, a distinctive period of Black Nationalism emerged. While nationalist sentiments were generally present throughout the Black experience in America, nationalism tended "to be most pronounced when the Negroes' status had declined or when they had experienced intense disillusionment following a period of heightened but unfulfilled expectations" (Bracey, Meier, Rudwick).

The period of the American Revolution between 1790 and 1820 lent itself to ideas of racial egalitarianism. Several Northern states and upper Virginia took steps to manumit their slaves. Beginning about 1800, the Baptist and Methodists made simplified appeals to lower classed Whites, who were socially excluded from the middle classes. The message of the evangelists held that Christ died for all, regardless of race or social condition. Responding to the message of the evangelists, Blacks flocked to the Baptist and Methodist churches which then enabled them to enjoy some degree of White acceptance.

By 1787 the prospect for African-Americans changed drastically. With its recognition of slavery, the United States Constitution set the tone for future discriminatory laws and devices. Baptist and Methodist Movements, hitherto relatively egalitarian in spirit, began to exclude and segregate their Black parishioners. In this context of legal slavery and declining status, the initial tendency towards Black Nationalism emerged. With a sense of alienation, African-Americans began developing separate institutions with predominately Black churches and denominations, fraternal organizations, and mutual aid societies coming into being. There was also a small contingent of African-Americans who proposed emigrating to Africa (H. S. Harris, 1972).

During the last two decades before the Civil War, a second period of Black Nationalism emerged. There were several key developments that spawned the growth of Nationalism:

The essential failure of the antislavery movement to liberate the slaves. . .the evidences of racism among White abolitionists who failed to accord Negroes positions of real influence in the antislavery societies, increasing trends toward disfranchisement and segregation in public accommodations in many of the Northeastern states, combined with the continuing pattern of discrimination in the Old Northwest that made. . .conditions there similar to that in the south; and the growing hopelessness of the economic situation. . . . At the same time, the compromise in 1850, with its new and more rigorous fugitive slave law, the Kansas-Nebraska Act, and the Dred Scott Decision, all made the outlook bleaker than ever. (Bracey, Meier, and Rudwick).

The gains of the Civil War and Reconstruction brought a sense of optimism to Black Americans. Blacks were freed, awarded citizenship, and given the right to vote through constitutional amendments. Congressional legislation and Reconstruction provided a period of Black political participation and clout. While Black Nationalism did not totally disappear, there was a feeling of non-nationalism.

The abrupt close of Reconstruction and its attendant consequences rekindled an interest in Black Nationalism. Primarily because of the desertion of the federal government, Reconstruction ended in 1877. Between 1880 and 1900, Blacks were exposed to the disappointment of disfranchisement and the hostility of "Jim Crowism" and lynching. Blacks were generally excluded from the skilled trades in the urban centers and regulated to farm tenancy and sharecropping in the rural South. It was from this context of violence, racial hatred, and declining status that the third period of Black Nationalism developed. The ideas of racial solidarity, racial pride, and self-help were integral parts of the movement. There was also a renewed interest in separate institutions, especially educational and religious. In addition, several leaders revived the idea of colonization.

Two prominent voices of this Black Nationalist period were Alexander Crummell and Henry McNeal Turner. Their speeches and writings overlap both the second and third periods of Black Nationalism. Because of Crummell's intellectual abilities he was called early in his life to join the Abolition Movement. In 1840, at age twenty-one, he began a life-long involvement with the anti-slavery crusade and other Black self-help projects.

Is it Necessary for the Black Nationalists to Address the Issues of Unmerited Oppression of Black People by Developing the Theodicies Which Make the Suffering Contextually Bearable?

The comparative process has revealed three important concepts. Believing that God would alleviate the slave condition through God's future actions, Garnet proposed the ideas of Providence and African-American Resistance. It was a two-dimensional approach that affirmed belief in God's Providence and simultaneous self-liberative activities. Not only did Garnet speak in terms of a spiritual-hope but a working-hope as well. He felt that the oppressed could never dispense with their own efforts for liberation.

Having set forth the theodicies of Garnet, Crummell, and Turner, in conclusion, the study focuses on the implications of their thoughts as they relate to a critically important issue: Is it necessary for the Black Nationalists to address the issues of the unmerited oppression of Black people by developing the theodicies which makes the suffering contextually bearable? The critical examination of this important issue is fundamentally dependent on the Black Nationalists' definition of self and the theistic-atheistic starting points: whether there is belief in God, what are the understandings of the God idea, and what are the desired relationships between God and persons and their relationships to each other?

Central in the thinking of Garnet, Crummell, and Turner was their belief in an all-good and all-powerful God. They came to know their true personhood through their conversion experiences that provided theistic affirmation. Having met God, the three men were transformed from lives of sin and feelings of worthlessness to new creatures liberated from sin, complete with value and meaning in their lives. The God-encounter provided the fundamental basis upon which the three men affirmed themselves and other

African-Americans as authentic human beings. Thus the ideas of God-given personhood and the universal brotherhood and sisterhood of humankind were extremely important.

Once identifying the three men's theistic starting points, then the answer to the first question is an obvious and resounding: No! Cone raises the important question: "[h]ow do we explain our faith in God as the liberator of the oppressed when Black people have been oppressed for more than three centuries in North America?"[1] Based, thus, on the Garnet-Crummell-Turner models of Black Nationalism in relation to God's justice, a serious Black Nationalist focuses on the questions posed by theodicy.

Having established the idea that a theistic Black Nationalist ought to have a theodicy, the conclusion turns to the thinking of the atheistic Black Nationalist. While an atheistic Black Nationalist has "no external living God to blame for the existence of evil," (M. Jones, 1987) if the atheistic Black Nationalist is to be taken seriously, he or she must take the God concept into account because religion is extremely important in the African-American experience. (1987). if the atheistic Black Nationalist is to be taken seriously, he or she must take the God concept into account because religion is extremely important in the African-American experience

---

[1] *God of the Oppressed*, 179.

"2020 & Still Waiting"
by Otis D. Alexander

From the first 23 Africans who arrived in Jamestown, Virginia, in 1619, the African experience has been an integral part of the American experience and has left its stamp on the country's institutions. The human relationship between the White economists and the Black population remains imbalanced and shaky. After all, the White power structure never accepted Africans as human beings. This not only demonstrated the ideology of White supremacy, but also represented a progressive economic system that lasted approximately 400 years.

African-Americans had always been denied rights by White plantation owners, even that of marriage to another slave. Their destiny was in the hands of others (Fishel & Quarles, 1967, p. 113). Free Blacks poured most of their energy, both emotional and spiritual, into the church, mainly the Baptist and Methodist denominations (p. 135). There were no other ways that Blacks and the vicious classicism that came along with dismantling the economic system of slavery that had brought great wealth to the White establishment.

More than a century after slavery, African-American continued to experience inequality, even after promises. Therefore, laws protecting Blacks were necessary for their further growth and development, and that of the country; New World Africans would no longer be an economic base.

Of course, because of White bigots' refusal to accept the newly free Black population, several federal civil rights laws were enacted during the newly free Black Reconstruction period. The Thirteenth Amendment abolished slavery in 1865. However, the terrorism from White bigots continued. In 1868, the Fourteenth Amendment affirmed citizenship for African-Americans under the Constitution. Two years later, in 1870, the Fifteenth Amendment provided that the right to vote could not be denied to United States citizens on the basis of "race, color, or previous condition of servitude."

The 1960s were a critical period for the Civil Rights Movement. It was the zenith of protest, radicalism, freedom train rides, marches, and demonstrations (Alexander, 2003, p. 518). In addition, President John F. Kennedy was assassinated, causing many African-American civil rights leaders to split over the most effective strategies to employ to address the federal government's refusal to enforce existing civil rights laws in this period. All of these activities led to the Civil Rights Act of 1964.

Even though the Civil Rights Act of 1964 was needed to address discrimination and bigotry against African-Americans, it was only a temporary relief of the tension between the unprogressive Whites and African-Americans, giving the former time to regroup for future discrimination. The passing of the act was probably expedited to stop protests and stall the legal system, while identifying a subtle manner of fairly sharing "the pursuit of happiness" with Blacks in the United States. The act has not been monitored and pushed to its limits in order to dismantle systematic racism/classicism.

While laws do not demonstrate everything about people's behavior, they do tell us what kinds of behavior a given society values- what it permits and even encourages (p. 246). Of course, during the 1960s, civil rights leaders had an accurate understanding of this, as did President John F. Kennedy. In his "Message to Congress" on February 28, 1963, President Kennedy stated that,

> The Negro baby born in America today...
>   Has about one-half as much chance to
>   Completing high school as a white baby
>   Born in the same place..., one third as
>   much chance as completing college,
>   one third as much chance of
>   becoming a professional man; twice
>   as much chance of becoming unemployed...,
>   a life expectancy, which is seven years
>   less, and prospects of earning half
>   as much (Fishel, 1967, p. 514).

This statement was a clear sign that White leaders in the United States knew that it was unjust, cruel, and vicious that the nation allowed African-Americans to be subjected to an inferior level of citizenship. President Kennedy went on to say,

> The right to vote is the most powerful
> and precious right in the world. This
> is a right that should not be denied on
> the grounds of race or color. Also, this
> is one of the greatest stepping-stones to

achieving other rights of citizenship...it
is not merely because of the Cold War,
and not merely because of the economic
waster of discrimination, which we are
committed to achieving true equality of
opportunity. The basic reason is because it
is right (p. 514).

Kennedy's appeal to conscience still did not forestall denial of James Meredith's entry to the University of Mississippi in 1961-1962, despite a US Supreme Court ruling in his favor (Lindsey, 1994, p. 122). It also did not deter Governor George C. Wallace of Alabama from personally blocking the entrance of the University of Alabama's auditorium to keep Vivian Malone Jones and James A. Hood from enrolling. Again, President Kennedy ordered the Alabama National Guard to remove the governor so that these two young students could register the same as the White university students (Hebel, 2004, A24).

In 1963, when Robert Kennedy, Sr. was the US attorney General, he noted that outside of Africa, "the only places on the planet known not to provide free public education are Communist China, North Vietnam, Sarawak, Singapore, British Honduras- and prince Edward County, Virginia" (Nussbaum & John-Hall, 2004, p. A8). He also chatted with civil rights marchers in the nation's capital and decried discrimination in hiring. However, he did not endorse the idea of affirmative action (Lindsey, 1994, p. 121).

The Civil Rights Act of 1964 assisted in dismantling a system that violated human rights. If this is true and done with a clean heart, then why are we still awaiting and protesting for justice in 2020?

While there were some noticeable gains from the Civil Rights Act of 1964, White leaders, Democrats and Republicans, who could make a real change, refuse. None of them wants to share the power of being equal. They do not want to dismantle structural racism/classicism. That is one of the reason that the Civil Rights act of 1964 is not always monitored. However, we must keep in mind that the qualities needed for peace, acceptance, and equality come out of the human consciousness. There is not any law in place, nor will there ever be, that can force human acceptance.

SELECTED AFRICAN PROVERBS

Father be careful, I'm in your path.

He that beats the drum for the mad man to dance is no better than the mad man himself.

You cannot say it is a clear day at night.

If you are filled with pride, then you will have no room for wisdom.

It takes a village to raise child.

When the elephants fight, the grass is destroyed.

A person with too much ambition cannot sleep in peace.

A bird that flies off the earth and lands on an anthill is still on the ground.

back does not break from bending. A back does not break from bending.

A beautiful thing is never perfect.

A blow to another's purse is like a blow to a mountain of sand.

A borrowed coat does not keep one warm.

A camel does not tease another camel about his humps.

A man's ruin lies in his tongue.

A monkey is a gazelle in its mother's eyes. A monkey is a gazelle in its mother's eyes

A person with a wound on his head keeps touching it.

You cannot build a house for last year's summer.

Where water is the boss there the land must obey.

No matter how beautiful and well-crafted a coffin might look, it will not make anyone wish for death.

When the shepherd comes home in peace, the milk is sweet.

To try and to fail is not laziness.

If you offend, ask for a pardon; if offended forgive.

A person with too much ambition cannot sleep in peace.

A spider's cobweb isn't only its sleeping spring but also its food trap.

If you do not have patience you cannot make beer.

He who runs after good fortune runs away from peace.

Teeth do not see poverty.

You have little power over what's not yours.

If you pick up one end of the stick you also pick up the other.

Show me your friends and I'll tell you who you are?

Do not follow a person who is running away. —
An orphaned calf licks its own back.

Better little than too little.

You must attend to your business with the vendor in the market, and not to the noise of the market.

When you befriend a chief remember that he sits on a rope.

The night has ears.

The child you sired hasn't sired you.

A doctor who invoked a storm on his people cannot prevent his house from destruction.

An intelligent enemy is better than a stupid friend.

The young bird does not crow until it hears the old ones.

If you carry the egg basket do not dance.
Prepared food has no master.

The worlds of the elders do not lock all the doors; they leave the right door open.
Even the best cooking pot will not produce food.

The child of a rat is a rat.

Where you will sit when you are old shows where you stood in youth.

He who is unable to dance says that the yard is stony.

When the roots of a tree begin to decay, it spreads death to the branches.

Slander by the stream will be heard by the frogs.

Even the lion, the king of the forest, protects himself against flies.

A flea can trouble a lion more than a lion can trouble a flea.

Wisdom is like a baobab tree; no one individual can embrace it.

The death of an elderly man is like a burning library. Anger and madness are brothers.

He who burns down his house knows why ashes cost a fortune.

Birds sing not because they have answers but because they have songs.

If your only tool is a hammer, you will see every problem as a nail.

When you show the moon to a child, it sees only your finger.

It is crooked wood that shows the best sculptor.

One who bathes willingly with cold water doesn't feel the cold.

Be a mountain or lean on one.

He who refuses to obey cannot command.

A single stick may smoke, but it will not burn.

Seeing is different than being told.

CONTRIBUTORS

Adegbite Adebimpe, born in the ancient Yoruba city of Ile-Ife, received the Bachelor of Arts degree in English from Obafemi Awolowo University. In addition, he holds the Master of Arts degree in Linguistics from Syracuse University and is a doctoral fellow in Linguistic Anthropology in the Department of Anthropology at Tulane University. As a Fulbright Scholar, Adebimpe taught indigenous languages at Florida Memorial University.

(Courtesy Blair E. Alexander, Sr.)

Blair E. Alexander, Sr. received his undergraduate education from Saint Augustine's University and the Master of Business Administration degree from the American University. In addition, he earned the Master of Divinity and Doctor of Ministry degrees from Howard University. Alexander retired from the United States Army at the rank of Lt. Colonel.

(Courtesy Brandon Trent Alexander)

Brandon Trent Alexander was born in Norfolk, Virginia. However, he grew up in Historic Berkley. He graduated from Lake Taylor Senior High School in the city. He received the Bachelor of Science in Accounting from Saint Augustine's University. Brandon is a licensed Real Estate Broker and a Developer.

(Courtesy Mark S. Askew, Sr.)

Ayana A. Askew has been writing and reciting poetry from an early ae. She is a junior at Historic Booker T. Washington High School in Norfolk, Virginia and also attends the Governor's School for the Arts in Theater. Askew is a Gold medalist in the 2020 111th NAACP National Convention ACT-SO Competition representing Norfolk, a 2018 House of Delegates Page for the Commonwealth of Virginia, a two-time first place winner of Norfolk's Southside Speaking Contest, and was selected as a runner-up for the "National August Wilson Competition" in New York in 2020.

(Courtesy Vanassa Araujo)

Vanassa Araujo, who is bilingual, was born in Bronx, New York of Dominicana heritage. However, she resides in Raleigh, North Carolina. Araujo attended Walton High School in the Bronx. She holds several professional licenses.

(Courtesy Askhat Aubakirov)

Askhat Aubakirov is a student of Biological Sciences at Kozybaev University (Petropavlovsk, Kazakhstan), and Vytautas Magnus University (Kaunas, Lithuania), was born in 1997, in Yavlenka village, Esil province, North Kazakhstan area, Republic of Kazakhstan. He grew up in a family of five children, and he was the third. Also, he attended a small village school, graduating in 2015 with high honors. Afterward, he moved to Petropavlovsk city to continue education with an interested in science and practical impact. In 2015, he began studies at North Kazakhstan Medical College (Petropavlovsk, Kazakhstan) and graduated in 2018 as a physician's assistant. He continued at the Kozybaev University (Petropavlovsk, Kazakhstan). During the 2019-2020 academic year, Aubakirov studied at Vytautas Magnus University (Kaunas, Lithuania) with a double major in biology and genetics. In addition, he successfully completed the Training on Science

Communication held by Cheltenham Festivals (Nur-Sultan, Kazakhstan).

A web and logo design freelancer in various projects, in 2019, Aubakirov was awarded second-place winner of FameLab Kazakhstan National Final competition organized by the British Council as well as the first-place winner of the Republican Olympiad on foreign languages (English) by L. N. Gumilyov Eurasian National University (Nur-Sultan, Kazakhstan).

Otis D. Alexander

(Courtesy Freddie Barnes)

Freddie I. Barnes, an ordained minister with a Doctor of Divinity degree, **is** the Clinical Chaplain at Edgecombe Youth Development Center in Rocky Mount, North Carolina. He oversees a program of social, religious, and cultural enrichment for the male juveniles at Edgecombe. Additionally, Barnes is the Prison Rape Elimination Act (PREA) Compliance Manager at Edgecombe that oversees the Edgecombe Facility's policies, practices and protocols for PREA compliance. He is a certified General Instructor who teaches and trains staff and juveniles in the Department of Public Service system. A recipient of numerous awards, Barnes is a retired chaplain officer in the United States Naval Reserves at the rank of Lieutenant Commander.

Felicia A. Andrews Bryant, born February 20, 1950, is a lifelong citizen of Gary, Indiana. Upon graduating from high school in 1967, she attended Ball State University. She married her husband Tyrone Bryant and had a family of five wonderful children.

For five years, Bryant taught preschoolers. Afterward, she was hired by her former high school as a library assistant and worked part-time with the Gary Public Library. She spent twelve years at GPL, retiring as Circulation Services Manager. Some of her hobbies include; sewing, writing,

From1995 to 1997, Bryant was an American Cancer Society Reach to Recovery Volunteer. In 1997, she became the Northwest Indiana coordinator for Reach to Recovery where and remained in this position for several years. However, she left to care for her father, an electrician, who was stricken with Alzheimer's. She continues to assists families who have loved ones with cancer, stroke, and or Parkinson's. This has become her life's contribution.

(Courtesy Panta X)

Neal Carrington was born in New York. However, he was reared on the island of St. Croix by indigenous Crucian parents. From a family of stellar musicians, Carrington began his music studies in the fifth grade with the trumpet. A former music teacher, he has performed with numerous Reggae ensembles, including Quiet Fire and has performed internationally. For thirty years, he has been based in Columbus, Ohio.

(Courtesy Muriel Cauthen)

Muriel "Myrrh" Cauthen, a playwright, actor, director, producer, and painter, was born in Philadelphia, Pennsylvania and reared in Norfolk, Virginia. She received the Bachelor of Arts degree in journalism, English, and drama from Livingstone College. Cauthen earned the Master of Science in Library Science degree from Atlanta University School of Library & Information Studies. Her art has been exhibited in Washington, DC and in Cairo, Luxor, and Aswan, Egypt with the International Artist Support Group.

(Courtesy Hamza Chafki)

Hamza Chafki was born and reared in the city of Oued Zem, Morocco. He received the Bachelor of Arts degree in Applied Linguistics and literature from the Faculty of Letters and Humanities of Sultan Moulay Slimane University and at Mohamed V University in Rabat. He is pursuing a Master of Arts degree in literary studies and cultural encounters at Sultan Moulay Slimane University. In addition, Chafki has been an English as a Second Language teacher at the high school level. In 2017, He was a Fulbright Scholar at Mercy College.

Photographer unknown
Imagine Ownership: Public Domain

Nancy Cunard, a journalist of the Harlem
Renaissance and an advocate of racial equality, was
born in 1896 in Leicestershire, England. Educated in
private institutions in London, Germany and Paris,
she founded of the Hours Press in the 1920s. In 1934,
Cunard published *Negro: An Anthology*. She died in
Paris in 1965.

(Courtesy Janet Darby)

Janet Darby, a farmer and Alchemist, was born in Washington, DC and reared in Danville, Virginia. She graduated from George Washington High School and received the Associate of Arts degree from Danville Community College.

Darby, who often sales her homemade remedies at the local farmer's market, is also an insurance sales representative.

(Courtesy Janell Davis)

Janell Davis was born and reared in Aikens, South Carolina. She is an Alumna of Saint Augustine's University. An avid reader, traveler, and devoted mother, who has a spent significant time in Cuba, rushes home to be with her sons Blake and Jules.

Photographer unknown
Imagine Ownership: Public Domain

Paul Laurence Dunbar, born in Dayton, Ohio in 1872, was the African-American poet of national recognition to earn a living from his literary work. An Alumnus of Howard University, he authored several novels, books, librettos, songs, essays, short stories, and six volumes of poetry. Dunbar transitioned in 1906.

Otis D. Alexander

(Courtesy Adrienee Dungee Felton)

John Riley Dungee I, an attorney by training, a master of the English language, and an education activist, was born free in King William County, Virginia on April 14, 1860. However, he was reared in Norfolk. He married Flossie B. Wingfield Dungee and they were the parents of John Riley Dungee, II, Roger Benton Dungee, Sr., Doris Dungee Trotman, Helma Dungee, and Duval Dungee.

(Courtesy Nabil Eddoumi)

Nabil Eddoumi was born and reared in the Moroccan city of Bejaad. His undergraduate studies were completed at the Faculty of Letters and Humanities at Sultan Moulay Slimane University, Mohamed V University, and King Fahd School of Translation. In addition, Eddoumi successfully taught as a Fulbright scholar at Florida Memorial University.

Currently, he instructs English at Abdellah Guennoun High School in his hometown, and is the author of Investigating Metacognitive Awareness of Reading: The Case Study of Moroccan Third Year University Students.

Image Ownership: Fair use image

Jessie Redmon Fauset was born in 1882, in Camden County, New Jersey. However, she was reared in Philadelphia and died in 1961. She graduated from Philadelphia High School for Girls. She received the Bachelor of Arts degree in classical languages (summa cum laude) from Cornell University in 1909 and the Master of Arts degree in French from the University of Pennsylvania.

Fauset taught teach French at high schools in the Bronx, New York, Washington, DC, and Maryland. She made here spiritual transition in Philadelphia in 1961. Philadelphia, where she lived until her death on April 30, 1961.

Photographer Tony Arias
(Courtesy Cynthia Rochelle Hall)

Cynthia Rochelle Clarambeau Hall, a stellar violinist, was born in Eugene, Oregon, in 1961. However, she was reared in Silver Spring, Maryland. Hall studied music at Columbia Union College and, Union College in Nebraska, thus completing her degree in violin at Florida Memorial University. In addition, she holds a degree in Addiction Studies Counseling.

As a soloist, Hall has performed with the Henderson Symphony Orchestra in Nevada, principal violinist with Allegro Vivo Quinte, the string quartet, Grace

Notes and the Concert Master in Miami, Florida of the annual performance Oratorio Handel's oratorio, *The Messiah*, in collaboration with Florida Memorial University and Historic Hampton House.

She has also performed with the Hallandale Pops Orchestra, Sugar Pops Orchestra as Assistant Concert Master, Symphony Delrey, Miami Lyric Orchestra, and Miami Lyric Opera. She is the spouse of Concert Pianist and Conductor, Dr. Nelson Hall.

(Courtesy William Ashanti Hobbs, II)

William Ashanti Hobbs, II, lyricist, playwright, screenwriter, was reared in Atlanta, Georgia. He received his undergraduate degree from Florida A & M University as well as the Master of Arts and Doctor of Philosophy degrees from Florida State University. Hobbs' area of concentration is Creative Writing and African-American Literature. Hobbs has taught English Composition & Rhetoric, fiction writing, poetry, and Literature of the Harlem Renaissance. He has been faculty at Florida State University, John Tyler Community College, Tallahassee College, and Virginia State University. Currently, Hobbs serves as the chairperson of the Visual & Performing Arts Department at Florida Memorial University.

(Courtesy James Arthur Holmes)

James Arthur Holmes, a distinguished Dr. Martin Luther King, Jr. Scholar, former Captain-Chaplain of the United States Army, currently teaches Church History at the Shaw University School of Divinity. He was born in Charleston, South Carolina. He received the Bachelor of Arts degree from Allen University and earned the Master of Divinity degree for the Interdenominational Theological Center. In addition, Holmes holds the Sacred Doctorate and the Doctor of Philosophy degrees from Boston University.

Holmes, who teaches from his research, is the author of Black *Nationalism and Theodicy: Emphasizing Henry Highland Garnet, Alexander Crummell, and Henry McNeal Turner*.

(Courtesy Browne Pamela Jafari)

Pamela Browne Jafari was born in Washington, DC. A member of Delta Sigma Theta Sorority, Inc. and an Alumna of Boston University, Jafari has been writing poetry and performing her work throughout the District of Columbia metropolitan area as well as in Ghana, West Africa. She has acted with Serenity Players Theatre Company, DC Playback &Synergy Playback, and the DC Community Playback Theatre Company.

Photographer unknown
Image Ownership: Public Domain

Georgia Douglas Johnson, one of the leading writers of the Harlem Renaissance, was born in Atlanta, Georgia, in 1877. She holds the Bachelor of Arts degree from Atlanta University in 1896, and studied piano at Oberlin Conservatory of Music in 1902. She published four volumes of poetry and wrote more than twenty-eight plays, including Blue Eyed Black Boy (1930). Johnson passed in 1966.

(Courtesy Argarita Johnson-Palavicini)

Argarita Johnson-Palavicini, born and reared in New York, is an internationally acclaimed flautist, vocalist, composer, and pedagogist. She has performed in Italy, Poland, Barbados, Finland, and most recently, Melbourne, Australia. She received the Bachelor of Music degree in Classical Flute Performance from Stetson University as well as the Master of Music degree in Jazz Studies from Indiana University Jacobs School of Music. Besides, Johnson-Palavicini earned the Doctor of Musical Arts degree in Studio & Vocal Jazz Performance from the University of Miami Frost School of Music.

Johnson-Palavicini, also an Assistant Professor of Music and Director of the Ambassador Chorale at Florida Memorial University.

Photography Otis D. Alexander
(Courtesy Belema Josiah)

Belema Josiah, the daughter of Nigerian parents, was reared in Miami. After graduating with honors from North Miami Beach Senior High School, and leaving a legacy in the theatre department and the jazz combo ensemble, she matriculated Florida Memorial University. As a music major, she joined several organizations, including the Obsidian Order Theatre Ensemble and Chamber Ensemble. In addition, Josiah has performed original choreopoems as well as works of her cultural surroundings as an African in the diaspora.

Photography C'est si Bon Studios
(Courtesy Keith Randall Knatt, II)

Keith Randall Knatt, II was reared and educated in Dallas, Texas. He received the Bachelor of Arts degree from Jarvis Christian College, a Master of Arts degree the University of Texas at Dallas, and the Master of Library & Information Science from The University of North Texas. Knatt is the author of *Assessing Needs for Academic Libraries: Emphasis on Jarvis Christian College.*

Knatt has been an instructor at Texas College and a librarian with the Miami Dade Public Library. He is a member of the Alpha Phi Alpha Fraternity, Inc.

(Courtesy Barry Koplen)

Barry Koplen, poet, writer, educator, entrepreneur, is a prize-winning photographer. He received the Bachelor of Arts degree from Emory University and the Master of Arts in Teaching degree from Converse College. In addition, he earned the terminal Master of Fine Arts degree from Queens University. In addition, he has long been writing poetry that is often published by friendly journals. Not long ago, Koplen published *Whale of Grief, Wail of Joy*. It is a book that has related his impressions life as a Jew in a non-Jewish world. This work is in addition to his numerous writings. His one act comedy, *Apples and Orange*, has been produced at the Wilton, CT Playhouse.

Koplen has taught Creative Writing, Humanities, and English at Danville Community College. Besides, he has owned and managed Abe Koplen Clothing Company in Danville, Virginia for more than two decades.

(Courtesy Helen D. Laurence)

Helen D. Laurence graduated from Andrew Jackson High School in her home town of Cambria Heights in the borough of Queens, New York. She received a Bachelor of Arts degree from Radcliffe College, Master of Education degree from Harvard University, and the Doctor of Education degree from the University of Massachusetts at Amherst. During graduate school at Amherst, she started doing yoga and moved into an Ashram where she met and married her husband Scott. Together they moved to St. Croix where Scott's family lived, and Helen worked as a librarian first at the University of the Virgin Islands and then at Florence Williams Public Library in Christiansted. Laurence is a co-founder of the Women's Coalition of St. Croix. Their son

335

Matthew was one of the first babies born in the new hospital that was subsequently destroyed by Hurricane Hugo. After 12 years, they moved to south Florida to be near Laurence's mother. The plan was to stay a couple of years and then relocate to the Pacific Northwest. Thirty-five years later, they still live in Palm Beach County. "Man plans, God laughs." In order to continue working as a professional librarian, Helen went back to school, received the Master of Library Science degree from the University of South Florida, and retired after nearly 25 years as an academic librarian at Florida Atlantic University. After retirement, they traveled to visit their son and daughter in law working overseas in Helsinki, Munich, Abu Dhabi and Stockholm. Their dream was to sell their house and possessions and live the nomadic life in their travel trailer. The current pandemic has delayed and possibly derailed those plans; they have focused for the duration on the inner journey.

Laurence is the joint author of *Academic Research on the Internet: Options for Scholars & Libraries.*

(Courtesy Frances M. Laveau)

Frances M. Laveau was born in Mobile, Alabama. She resides in Norfolk, Virginia. Besides, writing and reciting her works, Laveau spends a tremendous amount of time in her garden. She insists that she is just a dabbler in the Arts and enjoys escaping inwardly…becoming intoxicated and entertained by her thoughts without an expensive cover charge.

(Courtesy André Licencier)

André Licencier was born and reared in Miami, Florida in December 1978 and reared in Miami, Florida. However, his family is indigenous of
Haïti and The Bahamas. He graduated from Miami Edison Senior High School and has been working with the Miami Dade Public Library System for two decades. Licenser's hobbies are riding motorcycles and kayaking,

(Courtesy Winifred "Oyoko" Loving)

Winifred "Oyoko" Loving was born in the Boston, Massachusetts. The daughter of a minister was educated in the Boston Public Schools and received the Bachelor of Arts degree from Newton College of the Sacred Heart, and the Masters of Science in Education from Wheelock College. After graduate school, Loving relocated to the Caribbean island of St. Croix and taught elementary school there for 31 years, during which time she published two books of poetry, *Remember When* and *Spontaneous*.
In 1984, Loving taught school in London with the Fulbright Teacher Exchange Program. Loving she is known locally

339

for her live poetry readings. Her works have appeared in the *Bay State Banner*, the *St. Croix Avis*, the *Daily News*, *The VOICE*, *The Caribbean Writer*, *Poets and Writers*, and *Cosmopolitan Magazine*. After retiring, Loving published two illustrated children's storybooks; *My Name is Freedom* and *My Grandma Loves to Play.*

(Courtesy Linda Jones Malonson)

Linda Jones Malonson, a writer and entrepreneur, was born in Sunflower County, Mississippi in 1948. She is the tenth child in a family of thirteen, and loss her mother at the age of eleven. She spent years living in dysfunctional and received very little public schooling. However, she began writing out her pain and anguish at an early age as a way of maintaining her sanity.

341

Malonson vividly recalls when she was approaching age thirteen, and living with Mother Mary Tucker and her aunt, Susie Perkins, during the civil rights movement, when one night the Ku Klux Klan came looking for the late Mrs. Fannie Lou Hamer, and she had to hide under the bed.

Linda's life, like many abused children, was hard. She has since become a wife, a mother of five, and has grand and great-grandchildren. She lived most of her life between Mississippi and Texas. Currently, Malonson resides with her husband, in Richmond, Texas. She has authored more than 30 books.

(Courtesy Michael Darnell Marks, II)

Michael Darnell Marks, II, the son of a school teacher, was reared in the Hampton Roads and graduated from Lake Taylor Senior High School, Norfolk, Virginia. He received the Bachelor of Science degree in Business from Saint Augustine's University.

(Courtesy Julius E. McCullough)

Julius E. McCullough, Clarinetist, Composer, Conductor, Vocalist, is a graduate of Norfolk State College, now, Norfolk State University and has continued his study of music at Temple University, thus receiving a Master of Music degree from Virginia State College.

McCullough has taught in the public schools of North Carolina, Virginia and the District of Columbia. He has been the Director of Band and Chair of the Performing Arts Department at the Franklin Learning Center High School for Creative and Performing Arts, Philadelphia School District, Pennsylvania, where he directed the acclaimed Franklin Learning Center Jazz Ensemble and the 89 voice

Franklin Learning Center Concert Choir. After retiring from the Philadelphia School District, he accepted the position of Professor of Bands at St. Paul's College, Virginia.

A Charter Member of Epsilon Zeta Chapter of Kappa Alpha Psi Fraternity, Inc., McCullough has toured and performed with Duke Ellington and his Orchestra in the performances of his "Sacred Concerts," is currently the Artistic Director of the Boys Choir of Hampton Roads.

Photographer unknown
Image Ownership: Public Domain

Claude McKay was born Festus Claudius McKay in 1889 in Clarendon Parish, Jamaica. The author of numerous award-winning books, *Banjo* (1929) and *Banana Bottom* (1933), McKay studied at Tuskegee Institute and Kansas State University. He was one of the leading writers of the Harlem Renaissance as well as the Négritude Movement. He died in 1948 in Chicago, Illinois.

(Courtesy Yuri Millien)

Yuri Millien, a painter, sculptor, playwright, was born in Nassau, Bahamas in 1983, of a Haïtien mother. He is a graduate of Abaco Central High School on the island of Abaco. In addition to writing poetry, Millien is a rap artist.

Photographer - Matt Bell
(Courtesy Fred Motley)

Fred Motley, Master Storyteller, playwright, was born in 1950 in Danville, Virginia. He received the Bachelor of Arts degree from Barber-Scotia College in Concord, North Carolina. He is the recipient of an Honorary Doctorate of Human Letters for Storytelling from Living Epistle Bible College in Brown Summit, North Carolina.

Motley, who is a celebrated storyteller, has collaborated with the Danville Museum of Fine Arts and History. He has devoted his life to teaching others about African American history, dance and music. Motley is the author of several publications.

Image Ownership: Public Domain

Georgette Norman, a playwright, director, storyteller, lecturer, actor, dancer, was reared in Montgomery, Alabama. She received the Bachelor of Arts degree in history from Fisk University and the Master of Arts degree from Hampton University. She has taught at the University of the Virgin Islands, Auburn University, and the Virgin Islands Department of Education. Norman retired as the first Director of Troy University Rosa Parks Museum, Montgomery. In addition, Norman has directed and performed throughout the Caribbean and the United States.

(Courtesy Shirley White Smith Nottingham)

Shirley White Smith Nottingham was reared in the Campostella section of Norfolk, Virginia and graduated from the historic Booker T. Washington High School, where she also played trombone in its Marching Band. She enrolled in Hampton Institute, thus receiving the Bachelor of Arts degree. At Hampton, Nottingham pledged Gamma Theta Chapter of Alpha Kappa Alpha Sorority, Inc.in 1956 and remains a life member with Iota Omega Chapter. She has also pursued advanced studies at Norfolk State University and Old Dominion University. A retired educator with the Norfolk Public School System, Nottingham is currently treasurer of the Tidewater Area Musicians Branch of the National Association of Negro Musicians, Inc.

(Courtesy Diane Wilson Onwuchekwa)

Diane Wilson Onwuchekwa, born and reared in Danville, Virginia, has worked in the areas of pharmaceutical territory management, higher education sales and nonprofit administration. She spent more than two decades as pharmaceutical and medical center representative where she sold analgesics, diabetic and infectious disease medications. Her target audience was residents, fellows and attending physicians in teaching hospitals in the District of Columbia, Maryland, Ohio, Pennsylvania, and Virginia. She sold pharmaceuticals for Upjohn, Berlex, Fujisawa, and Whitehall Labs.

A Hampton University alumna, Onwuchekwa earned a Master of Arts degree in Adult Education from North Carolina A&T State University.

(Courtesy Erick Payan)

Erick Payan, the CEO, Founder, and Content Editor at Carnival Cruise Line Miami Blog, was born in Guantánamo, Cuba, in 1973. At the age of 20, he immigrated to the United States and now resides in Miami.

The father of two amazing daughters, Payan started writing poems in 1991 and was inspired by personal experiences and life's reality. He has written more than 80 poems. His relative, the renowned Spanish poet and playwright, Federico Garcia Lorca, influenced his writing.

(Courtesy Arthur Petersen)

Arthur Petersen was born in Bronx, New York City and reared in Christiansted, Virgin Islands. He graduated from St. Croix Central High School and received the Associate of Arts degree from Clinton College. Petersen was declared as the first Virgin Islander to represent South Carolina in the Legislative Black Caucus during his tenure at Clinton. Currently, he is employed with the Virgin Islands Department of Education where he has been for seventeen years.

(Courtesy Cipriani A. Phillip, Jr.)

Cipriani A. Phillip, Jr. is a Crucian native Virgin Islander whose government service began as a secondary education Mathematics instructor with the Virgin Islands Department of Education. He also spent over 20 years serving our nation in the armed forces. He continues his storied career as a recently minted cybersecurity analyst. He has recently begun a series of memoirs exploring the enhancement of pillars of our modern day society to include identifying root causes of issues, promulgating theories, solutions, and recommendations to complex, perplexing, and even vexing challenges of our day. Phillip's major research is "Storytelling, storytellers & Information Systems with Emphasis on the Virgin Islands."

(Courtesy Alvin Pondexter)

Alvin Pondexter was born in Tallahassee, Florida. However, he grew up in Miami. He received the Bachelor of Arts degree from Florida A&M University. In addition, Pondexter earned the Master of Arts and Master of Fine Arts degrees from the University of Wisconsin at Madison. He has taught Art at Florida International University and Florida Memorial University.

(Courtesy Julian Rolle)

Julian Rolle, poet, storyteller, wrier, was born in 1971 in Freeport, Bahamas. However, he has lived in Jamaica and New York. Rolle graduated from Hialeah Miami Lakes High School in 1989, where he was inspired to write from his English Teacher Mr. Boyd. Rolle's work has recited and performed throughout South Florida and Atlanta, Georgia.

(Courtesy Beryl A. Watson-Shaw)

Beryl A. Watson Shaw, Chemist, Researcher, Visiting Professor, is a sixth generation Crucian on her Father's maternal side. Her Great Great Grandfather, August Bough, an A M E. Minister was one of the founders of the A M E Church on St. Croix. In addition, her grandfather, James Bough, was appointed the District Attorney for the United States Virgin Islands by President Lyndon B. Johnson.

On the evening of St. Joseph's Catholic Central High School (1967) Graduation, on the island of St. Croix, Shaw was awarded an additional diploma from the

Catholic University of America. In the last semester of her senior year at Morgan State College (now University), she was recruited by Martin Marietta Research Laboratories (MML). Within a year, she was nominated for Martin Marietta's Silver Cup for research related to the St. Croix Martin Marietta Alumina Plant. Next, MML involved Shaw in the National Urban League's Black Executive Exchange Program (BEEP). Through this program, scientists who lectured at HBCU's titled of Visiting Professors. Shaw was the first BEEP industrial lecturer at Jackson State University. She also lectured at Southern University. Meanwhile, MML financed Shaw's Master of Arts degree at Antioch University.

(Courtesy Rose Mary Stiffin)

Rose Mary Stiffin was educated in Indianola, Mississippi — the Delta hometown of the blues legend, BB King. She has been published in numerous periodicals, including the *Imagine literary* magazine and the *Algonquin Quarterly*. A graduate of Mississippi Valley State University, Stiffin received the Master of Science degree in Organic Chemistry from Mississippi State University and earned the Doctor of Philosophy degree in biochemistry from the University of Tennessee. She is a professor at Florida Memorial University.

Otis D. Alexander

(Courtesy Jeffrey Dean Swain)

Jeffrey Dean Swain is the Dean of Campus Ministry in the Susie C. Holley Religious Center at Florida Memorial University. He is also an Assistant Professor of Criminal Justice. Swain is a *Phi Beta Kappa* graduate of Morehouse College and holds a Master of Science degree from Atlanta University. In addition, he earned the Juris Doctor degree from the University of Miami and Doctor of Philosophy degree from the Union Institute & University. Swain is the author of six books: *Black and Still Here, A World of Color, Education in America: A Dilemma in the 21ˢᵗ Century, The Soul Unsettled, The Poetry Café for Women and Ancestors of the African Diaspora: A Tribute in Prosetry*. His opinion column can be read regularly in the *South Florida Times*.

360

(Courtesy Onika M. Thomas)

Onika M. Thomas, a Concert Singer and dancer, was born and reared in Christiansted, Virgin Islands. She received the Bachelor of Science degree in Philosophy, graduating summa cum laude from Lincoln University of Pennsylvania. In addition, Thomas has studied at Southeastern University DC as well as the University of the District of Columbia. She studied voice with the renowned Charlotte Wesley Holloman and piano with Geraldine Haylett Thomas Boone and William Lockwood Howcott. She has performed as a recitalist in Washington, DC, Virginia, New Jersey, and the Virgin Islands. Thomas is a member of Phi Delta Kappa International.

Photographer Otis D. Alexander
(Courtesy Adele D. Allen)

Avicia B. Hooper Thorpe, writer, educator, pianist, was born in in Danville, Virginia and celebrated her 112th year birthday on April 14, 2020. A product of the public schools where she also walked three miles per day for an education, Thorpe received the Bachelor of Arts degree from Bluefield State University. Thorpe also did advanced studies at Michigan State University, Columbia University, and Virginia State University.

The Alpha Kappa Alpha Sorority, Inc. member has been writing poetry and prose since her childhood. Her work has been published throughout the Danville community. Thorpe, who was a friend of the renowned scientist, George Washington Carver, retired in 1966 from Danville's Langston High School as an English Teacher.

(Courtesy Dinizulu Gene Tinne)

Dinizulu Gene Tinne, a sculptor, painter, graphic designer, and linguist, was born in New York. He has been the principal artist in composing the work for the Key West African Cemetery Memorial Monument. His research has appeared in numerous peer review journals and books, including *Florida History Quarterly*, *Islas Bilingual*, *Journal of African-American History*, *Creative Wizards*, and *One Drop of Imagination: Embracing Selected Arts Energies*.

A recipient of numerous awards, Tinne received the 2013 African-American Achievers Award in Arts and Culture from Broward County-based JM Family Enterprises, Pillars Award from the Miami Dade Black Affairs Advisory Board, recognition by the Talladega College Alumni, and the United States Armed Forces Southern Command, a Miami ICON award. Tinne has been faculty at Florida Memorial University.

(Courtesy André M. Titus, Jr.)

André M. Titus, Jr. was born and reared in Christiansted, Virgin Islands of the United States. He received Bachelor of Science degrees in Health and Physical Education from York College of the City University of New York. CUNY. He is the heads Men's volleyball at York College. In addition, Titus is a Public Health Educator for the New York City Department of Health - BHIV.

(Courtesy Vertez Burks)

Lovel Toran Waiters was a gifted poet and essayist. She was born on November 28, 1950 in Norfolk, Virginia. An Alumna of Norfolk State University, she authored two books, *The Woman under the Hat* and *Right place Right Time*, a play, and organized and participated in poetry readings. She was a long-time member of the African-American Writer's & Artists, Inc. as well as the 1st vice-President of the National Council of Negro Women's Inc. San Diego Section ftom 1994-1995.

(Courtesy Thomas Walker II)

Thomas Walker II, the son of one of the first African-American physicians in South Florida, was born and reared in Fort Lauderdale. He attended Morehouse College. However, he received the Bachelor of Arts degree from Florida Memorial University. In addition, Walker pursued the graduate studies at Nova University. He is the author of African-*American Males & the Residual Effects of Slavery*.

367

Photography Spruilly Maehands
(Courtesy Ronald R. White)

Ronald Rodney White was born in 1972 in the Naval Hospital in Portsmouth, Virginia. However, he grew in the Campostella section of Norfolk and graduated from Lake Taylor Senior High School. White, a member of the Omega Psi Phi Fraternity, Inc., received the Bachelor of Science degree in business from Saint Augustine's University

(Courtesy AcNeal Williams)

AcNeal L. Williams was born on the island of Grand Bahama, The Bahamas. He graduated from the Grand Bahamas Catholic High School in Freeport and received the Bachelor of Arts degree in Voice Performance and finance, summa cum laude, from Florida Memorial University. In addition, Williams earned the Master of Music degree in Classical Voice Performance from Howard University.

Otis D. Alexander

(Courtesy Catherine I. Williams)

Catherine I. Williams is a highly sought after public and private sector advisor, educator, and training specialist. She has a Bachelor of Arts degree in French from Norfolk State University, a Master of Science degree in Urban Administration from Georgia State University, Master of Divinity degree from Virginia Union University and Doctor of Philosophy degree in Public Administration & Policy from University of Georgia. She works with faith-based communities, nonprofit organizations, and youth programs.

Photography Alice Boughton
Image Ownership: Public Domain

William Butler Yeats, poet, playwright, thespian, was born in Dublin, Ireland in, 1865. However, he was reared in Sligo and in London. Dublin's Erasmus Smith High School in 1881. He attended the Metropolitan School of Art. In 1922, Yeats was appointed Senator for the Irish Free State. A year later, he was awarded the Nobel Prize in Literature. He died in Menton, France in 1939.

(Courtesy David Zuber**)**

David Zuber is a retired educator residing in northern California. He received the Master of Science degree in psychology from Humboldt State University and the Master of Arts degree in African Studies from University of Birmingham, England, where he completed research regarding the social, cultural, political and economic developments in Africa and the Diaspora. In addition, Zuber has pursued postgraduate studies in counseling and educational administrative.

As an undergraduate, Zuber was an exchange student for a year at the University of Ghana at Legon. Later he taught at Cuttington University in Liberia for several years. He also served as a high school counselor and secondary school administrator in California for many years.

.

Resources

Aberson, C. L. and T.E. (2004). The aversive racism paradigm and responses favoring African Americans: Meta-analytic evidence of two types of favoritism. *Social Justice Research*, 17(1), 25-46.

Accapadi, M.M. (2007). When White women cry: How White women's tears oppress women of color. *College Student Affairs Journal*.

Adams, G. et al. (2008). Beyond prejudice: Toward a sociocultural psychology of racism and oppression. In G. Adams, M. Biernat, N. R. Branscombe, C. S. Crandall, & L. S. Wrightsman (Eds.), *Commemorating Brown: The Social Psychology of Racism and Discrimination* (pp. 215-246). Washington, DC: APA Books.

Adams, G. et al. (2006). Perceptions of racism in Hurricane Katrina: A Liberation Psychology analysis. *Analyses of Social Issues and Public Policy*, 6, 215-235.

Akerlof, G. A., and Rachel E. Kranton (2000), Economics and Identity, *Quarterly Journal of Economics* 115(3), 715–753.

Alexander, M. (2012). *The New Jim Crow: Mass Incarceration in the Age of Colorblindness*. The New Press.

Alexander, O.D. (2007). Blacks still not equal even after the Civil Rights Act of 1964. In M. Christopher Brown's *Still not equal: expanding educational opportunity in society*. New York: Peter Lang Publishing, Inc.

Alexander, O.D. (2019). *Redefining Moments: Négritude, Negrismo, Indigenismo & Harlem Renaissance.* New York: African Tree Press.

Alexander, O.D. (2003). Roy Wilkins. *Scribner encyclopedia of American lives: The 1960s.* New York: Gale.

Alexander, O.D. (2018). *Voicing Justice, Equality, and Freedom: Everybody's Business.* New York: African Tree Press.

Alfani, G. (2013). "Plague in seventeenth century Europe and the decline of Italy: and epidemiological hypothesis." *European Review of Economic History,* 17, 4 ,408-430

Alfani, G. and T. Murphy. (2017). "Plague and Lethal Epidemics in the Pre-Industrial World." *Journal of Economic History* 77 (1), 314–343.

Allen, R. C. (2001). "The Great Divergence in European Wages and Prices from the Middle Ages to the First World War." *Explorations in Economic History,* October.

Allen, R. C. et al. (2011). "Wages, prices, and living standards in China, 1738-1925: in comparison with Europe, Japan, and India." *Economic History Review,* vol. 64, 8-36.

Allen, R. C. et al. (2012). "The colonial origins of the divergence in the Americas: A labor market approach." *Journal of Economic History,* vol. 72, no. 4, December.

Allen, T. W. (1994). *The Invention of the White Race.* London: Verso.

Anderson, W. (2006). *The Cultivation of Whiteness: Science, Health and Racial Destiny in Australia*. Durham, NC: Duke University Press.

Angell, S. (1992). *Bishop Henry McNeal Turner and African-American Religion in the South*. Knoxville: University of Tennessee Press.

Álvarez Nogal, C. and Prados de la Escosura, L. (2013). 'The Rise and Fall of Spain (1270-1850)', Economic History Review, 66, 1, 1–37.

Andreeva, M. (2019). (Re)Shaping Political Culture and Participation Through Social Networks. *Journal of Liberty and International Affairs*, [online] 5(2), pp.43-54. Available at: <https://nbn-resolving.org/urn:nbn:de:0168-ssoar-64606-3> [Accessed 15 June 2020].

Apfelbaum, Norton, and Sommers. (2012). Racial color blindness: Emergence, practice, and implications. *Current Directions in Psychological Science.*

Apfelbaum, Sommers, and Norton (2008). Seeing race and seeming racist? Evaluating strategic colorblindness in social interaction. *Journal of Personality and Social Psychology*, 95, 918-932.

Apfelbaum, E.P. et al. (2010). In blind pursuit of racial equality? *Psychological Science*, 21, 1587-1592.

Armitage, R. (2020). Amid Black Lives Matter protests, a rumored Antifa invasion fueled fear in regional Idaho. <https://www.abc.net.au/news/2020-06-10/how-a-rumour-about-antifa-looters-fuelled-

fear-in-regional-usa/12334638> [Accessed 15 June 2020].

Ashley, K, and Lothwell, L. (2019) Black Lesbian, Gay, Bisexual, Transgender, and Queer Identities and Mental Health 139-150.

Baranov, Victoria, Ralph De Haas and Pauline Grosjean (2020), Men. Roots and Consequences of Masculinity Norms, CEPR Discussion Paper No. 14493, London.

Barksdale, k. and Kinnamon, R. (1972). Black Writers of America: A Comprehensive Anthology. New York: Macmillan Company.

Bell, D. (1987). *And We Are Not Saved: The Elusive Quest for Racial Justice.* New York, NY: Basic Books.

Bell, D. (1992). *Faces at the Bottom of the Well: The Permanence of Racism.* New York, NY: Basic Books.

Bonilla-Silva, E. (2003). *Racism without Racists: Color-Blind Racism and the Persistence of Racial Inequality in the United States.* Lanham, MD: Rowman & Littlefield.

Bracey, J. H. et al, (1970). *Black Nationalism in America.* New York, NY.: Bobbs-Merrill.

Brown, M. C. (2007). *Still not equal: expanding educational opportunity in society.* New York: Peter Lang Publishing, Inc.

Chisholm, A. (1979). *Nancy Cunard: A biography.* New York: Knopf.

Collins, P. H. (2000). *Black Feminist Thought: Knowledge, Consciousness, and the Politics of Empowerment. 2nd ed.* New York, NY: Routledge.

Cohen, P. (2019). "What Reparations for Slavery Might Look Like in 2019: The idea of economic amends for past injustices and persistent disparities is getting renewed attention. Here are some formulas for achieving the aim." *New York Times*, May 23.

Cone, J. H. (2011). *The Cross and the Lynching Tree*. Orbis Books.

Cooper, R. et al. (2012). The associations of clinicians' implicit attitudes about race with medical visit communication and patient ratings of interpersonal care. *American Journal of Public Health*, 102, 979-987.

Correll, J. et al. (2007). The influence of stereotypes on decisions to shoot. *European Journal of Social Psychology*, 37(6), 1102-1117.

"Coronavirus Will Change the World Permanently. Here's How." (2020). Politico, March 19. (Accessed August 29, 2020   from https://www.politico.com/news/magazine/2020/03/19/coro navirus-effect-economy-life-society-analysis-covid-135579).

Crocker, J. and Major, B. (2003). The self-protective properties of stigma: Evolution of a modern classic. *Psychological Inquiry*, 14(3&4), 232-237.

Crummell, A. (1882).   "The Destined Superiority of the Negro," in *The Greatness of Christ and Other Sermons,* (New York: Thomas Whittaker.

Čyževs'kyj, D. (1975). *A History of Ukrainian Literature*. Colorado: Littleton.

Daniels, J. (1997). *White Lies: Race, Class, Gender, and Sexuality in White Supremacist Discourse*. New York, NY: Routledge.

Davis, A. J. (2018). *Policing the Black Man: Arrest, Prosecution, and Imprisonment*. New York: Vintage Books.

Davis, A. Y. (2016). *Freedom Is a Constant Struggle: Ferguson, Palestine, and the Foundations of a Movement*. Chicago: Haymarket Books.

Diss, K. (2020). George Floyd's death shows the power of social media as the US continues to grapple with racial tensions. <https://www.abc.net.au/news/2020-05-28/minneapolis-george-floyd-protests-amplify-bad-us-race-relations/12294626> [Accessed 15 June 2020].

Dovidio, J. F. and Gaertner, S.L. (2004). Aversive Racism. *Advances in Experimental Social Psychology*, 36, 1-52.

Dovidio, J. F. and Gaertner, S.L. (2007). New directions in aversive racism research: Persistence and pervasiveness. In C. W. Esqueda (Ed.), *Nebraska Symposium on Motivation: Motivational aspects of prejudice and racism*, 43-67). New York: Springer.

Dovidio, J. F. et al. (2002). Why can't we just get along? Interpersonal biases and interracial distrust.

Cultural Diversity and Ethnic Minority Psychology, 8(2), 88-102. doi: 10.1037/1099-9809.8.2.88.

Dovidio, J. F. et al. (2002). Implicit and Explicit Prejudice and Interracial Interaction. *Journal of Personality & Social Psychology*, 82(1), 62-68.

Dovidio, J.F. et al. (2005) (Eds). *On the Nature of Prejudice: Fifty Years After Allport*. Malden, MA: Blackwell.

DuBois, W.E.B. (2003). *Darkwater: Voices from Within the Veil*. Amherst, NY: Humanity Books.

Du Bois, W.E.B. (1999). *The Souls of Black Folk: Authoritative Text, Contexts, Criticism*. New York: W.W. Norton.

Duncan, E. (2020). Brands are speaking up on Black Lives Matter. But are they taking action behind the scenes? <https://www.abc.net.au/news/2020-06-13/brands-on-black-lives-matter/12344476> [Accessed 15 June 2020].

Enflo, K. and Missiaia, A. (2018). "Regional GDP estimates for Sweden, 1571-1850." *Historical Methods*, 51, 115-137.

Enflo, K. et al. (2014). "Swedish regional GDP 1855-2000 Estimations and general trends in the Swedish regional system." *Research in Economic History*, 30, 47-89.

Fang, W. and Miller, S. (2014). Output Growth and its Volatility: The Gold Standard through the Great

Moderation. *Southern Economic Journal*, 80(3), 728-751.

Feagin, J.R. (2012). *White Party, White Government: Race, Class, and U.S. Politics*. New York: Routledge.

Feagin, J.R. (2010). T*he White Racial Frame: Centuries of Framing and Counter-Framing*. New York: Routledge.

Felice, E. (2018). 'The roots of a dual equilibrium: GDP, productivity, and structural change in the Italian regions in the long run (1871-2011)', *European Review of Economic History*.

Fine, M. et al. (1996). *Off White: Readings on Race, Power and Society*. New York: Routledge.

Fishel Jr., F. and B. Quarles. (967). *The Negro American: A documentary history*. New York: William Morrow.

Fulton, S. and T. Martin. *Rest in Power: The Enduring Life of Trayvon Martin*. New York: Spiegel & Grau.

Gilbert, M. (1992). *The Holocaust, Maps and Photographs*. New York: Braun Centre for Holocaust Studies.

Gilbert. (1993). *Atlas of the Holocaust*. New York: William Morrow and Company, Inc.

Gilman, S. and S. Katz, S. (1993). *Anti-Semitism in Times of Crisis*. New York: New York University Press.

Götz, A. (2008). *Hitler's Beneficiaries: Plunder, Racial war and the Nazi Welfare State*. New York: Holt.

Gross, J. T. (2001). Neighbors: The Destruction of the Jews of Jedwabne Poland. Princetown University Press: Oxford.

Giuliano, P. (2018). *Gender: A Historical Perspective, The Oxford Handbook of Women and the Economy*, Ed. Susan Averett, Laura Argys and Saul Hoffman. Oxford University Press, New York.

Grosjean, P. and R. Khattar (2019). It's Raining Men! Hallelujah? The Long-Run Consequences of Male-Biased Sex Ratios. *The Review of Economic Studies*, 86(2), 723–754.

Gutman, I. (1990). *Encyclopedia of the Holocaust*. New York: Macmillan.

Gutman, I. (1982). *The Jews of Warsaw 1939-1943: Ghetto, Underground, Revolt*. Bloomington, IN: Indiana University Press.

Gutman, Y. (1982). *The Warsaw Ghetto 1939-1943: Ghetto, Underground, Revolt*. Bloomington, IN: Indiana University Press.

Gutman, Y. (1994). *Resistance: The Warsaw Uprising*. Boston, MA: Houghton, Miffin Company.

Gutman, Y. and Gutterman, B. (2004). *The Auschwitz Album*. Jerusalem, Israel: Yad Vashem.

Halton, C. (2019). "Digital Native." Investopedia, July 19. Accessed August 29, 2020 from https://www.investopedia.com/terms/d/digital-native.asp).

Harris, H.S. (1972). *Paul Cuffee: Black America and the African Return*. New York, NY: Simon and Schuster.

Jones, M. (1987). *The Color of God: the Concept of God in Afro-American Thought*. Macon: Mercer University Press.

Hebel, S. (2004). Segregation's legacy still troubles campuses. *The Chronicle of Higher Education* 50 (36) May 14, p. A24.

Henig, R. M. (1992). "Flu Pandemic: Once and Future Menace. " *New York Times Magazine*, November 19.

Higdon, N. (2020). What is Fake News? A Foundational Question for Developing Effective Critical News Literacy Education. Democratic Communiqué, <https://eds.b.ebscohost.com/eds/pdfviewer/pdfviewer?vid=5&sid=ac3f8e3a-a57e-4e1e-abb9-81f8ba443506%40pdc-v-sessmgr04> [Accessed 15 June 2020].

Himmelstein, M.S. and Sanchez, D.T. (2016), Masculinity Impediments: Internalized Masculinity Contributes to Healthcare Avoidance in Men and Women. *Journal of Health Psychology*, 21, 1283–1292.

Hobson, K. (2017). " Feeling Lonely? Too Much Time On Social Media May Be Why." NPR, March 6. (Accessed August 29,2020 from https://www.npr.org/).

Hoehling, A. A. (1961). *The Great Epidemic.* Boston: Little Brown and Company.

Hughes, S. S. (1977). *The Virus: A History of the Concept.* New York: Heinemann Educational Books Ltd.

Hutchens, G. (202). Black Lives Matter protesters have unwittingly recorded the single largest outbreak of police brutality in US history. <https://www.abc.net.au/news/2020-06-07/police-brutality-caught-on-film-black-lives-matter/12330672> [Accessed 15 June 2020].

Jazeera, A. (2020). A timeline of the George Floyd and anti-police brutality protests. <https://www.aljazeera.com/news/2020/06/timeline-george-floyd-protests-200610194807385.html> [Accessed 13 June 2020].

Jenson, R. (2008). White privilege shapes the U.S. In P.S. Rothenberg's (Ed.) *White Privilege: Essential Readings on the Other Side of Racism,* pp. 129-132. New York: Worth.

Johns, M. et al. (2005). Knowing is Half the Battle: Teaching Stereotype Threat as a Means of Improving Women's Math Performance. *Psychological Science, 16*(3), 175-179.

Johnson, J. D. et al. (1995). Justice is still not colorblind: Differential racial effects of exposure to inadmissible evidence. *Personality and Social Psychology Bulletin, 21*(9), 893-898.

Jones, B. E. and Hill, M.J. (199). African American lesbians, gay men, and bisexuals. In *Textbook of homosexuality and mental health*, Edited by: Cabaj, R. P. and Stein, T. S. 549–561. Washington, DC: American Psychiatric Association.

Jones, J. M. (1998). Psychological knowledge and the new American dilemma of race. *Journal of Social Issues, 54*(4), 641-662.

Jones, J.M. (2005). Mechanisms for coping with victimization: Self-protection plus self-enhancement. In J. F. Dovidio, P. Glick, & L. A. Rudman (Eds.), *On the Nature of Prejudice: Fifty years after Allport* (pp. 155-171). Malden, MA: Blackwell.

Jones, J.M. et al. (2014). *The psychology of diversity.* United Kingdom: Wiley-Blackwell.

Leonardo, Z. (2009). *Race, Whiteness and Education.* New York: Routledge.

Lewis, D.L. (1997). *When Harlem Was in Vogue.* New York: Penguin Books.

Lindsey, H.O. (1994). *A history of Black America.* Greenwich, CT: Chartwell.

Lipsitz, G. (1998). *The Possessive Investment in Whiteness.* Philadelphia: Temple University Press.

Lopez, I.H. (2006). *White by Law: The Legal Construction of Race.* New York: NYU Press.

Low, S. (2009). "Maintaining Whiteness: The Fear of Others and Niceness." *Transforming Anthropology*, 17, (2): 79–92.

Low, W.A. and Clift, V.A. (1981). *Encyclopedia of Black America*. New York: McGraw-Hill.

Mahalik, J.R. et al. (2003). Development of the Conformity to Masculine Norms Inventory. *Psychology of Men & Masculinity*, 4(1), 3–25.

Major, B. and O'Brien, L. T. (2005). The Social Psychology of Stigma. *Annual Review of Psychology, 56*, 393-421.

Malveaux, J. Still at the periphery: The economic status of African Americans. In *Race and resistance: The economics of race, class and gender in the United States*, 291-296. South End Press.

Mantsios, G. (1999/2007). Media Magic: Making class invisible. In P. S. Rothenberg (Ed.), *Race, Class, and Gender in the United States* (7th ed., 636-644). New York: Worth.

Markus, H.R. and Moya, P.M. (2010). *Doing race: 21 essays for the 21st century*. New York, NY: W.W. Norton.

Martens, A. et al. (2006). Combating stereotype threat: The effect of self-affirmation on women's intellectual performance. *Journal of Experimental Social Psychology, 42*(2), 236-243.

Mays, V. M. et al. Race, Race-Based Discrimination, and Health Outcomes Among African Americans. *Annual Review of Psychology, 58*, 201-225.

McKay, C. (1970). *Banjo*. New York: Mariner Books.

McIntosh. (1988/2008). *White privilege: Unpacking the invisible knapsack.*

Miller. (1986/2007). Domination and subordination. In P. S. Rothenberg (Ed.), *Race, Class, and Gender in the United States* (7th ed., 123-130). New York: Worth.

Moorhead, M.C. (1973). *Mammon vs. history: American paradise or Virgin Islands home.* Frederiksted, VI: United People Party.

New African. (2018). "Recalling Africa's harrowing tale of its first slavers – The Arabs – as UK Slave Trade Abolition is commemorated." *New African*, March 3.

Nussbaum, P. and John-Hall, A (2004). Fight for school equality still leaves scars for many. *The Phildelphia Inquirer*, 175th Year, No. 347, May 12.

Ofari, E. (1972). *Let Your Motto Be Resistance: The Life and Thought of Henry Highland Garnet*. Boston: Beacon Press.

Pamuk, S. (2007). "The Black Death and the origins of the 'Great Divergence' across Europe, 1300-1600." *European Review of Economic History*, vol. 11, 2007,280-317.

Pamuk, S. (2016). "Economic Growth in Southeastern Europe and Eastern Mediterranean, 1820-1914." *Economic Alternatives*, No. 3.

Patanjali. (1953). *How to Know God: the Yoga Aphorisms of Patanjali*. New York: Harper.

Pullan, B. (1992). "Plague and Perceptions of the Poor in Early Modern Italy." In T. Ranger and P. Slack (eds.), *Epidemics and Ideas. Essays on the Historical Perception of Pestilence.* Cambridge: CUP, 101-23; Alfani, G., *Calamities and the Economy.*

Roche, L. (2008). *The Radiance Sutras: 112 Tantra Yoga Teachings for opening to the divine in everyday life.* Marina del Rey, CA: Syzygy Creations, Inc.

Rodney, W. (1981). *How Europe Underdeveloped Africa.* Washington, DC: Howard University.

Rosés, J. et al. (2010). 'The upswing of regional income inequality in Spain (1860–1930)', *Explorations in Economic History,* 47, 244-257.

Rosenberg, P. (2004). Color blindness in teacher education: An optical delusion (Chapter 19). In *Off White/Readings on Power, Privilege & Resistance*, 257-272). New York: Routledge.

Rosenthal, E. (2020). "A Health System Set up to Fail." *New York Times*, May 8, A29.

Rothenberg. P.S. (2008). *White Privilege: Essential Readings on the Other Side of Racism*. Worth Publishers.

Salgado, D.M. et al. (2019). Men's Health-Risk and Protective Behaviors: The Effects of Masculinity and Masculine Norms. *Psychology of Men & Masculinities*, 20(2), 266–275.

Salzberg, S. and J. Goldstein. (2001). *Insight Meditation Workbook*. Boulder, CO: Sounds True.

Sampson, R. J. and S.W. Raudenbush. (2004). Seeing Disorder: Neighborhood Stigma and the Social Construction of 'Broken Windows'. *Social Psychology Quarterly*, 67(4), 319-342.

Sardarizadeh, S. and Robinson, O. (2020). George Floyd protests: Twitter bans over #DC Blackout hoax.: <https://www.bbc.com/news/technology-52891149> [Accessed 15 June 2020].

Schor, J. (1977).*Henry Highland Garnet: A Voice of Black Nationalism in the Nineteenth Century*. Westport, CT: Greenwood Press.

Sears, D. O. (2004). A Perspective on Implicit Prejudice from Survey Research: Comment. *Psychological Inquiry, 15*(4), 293-297.

Sesko, A.K. and Biernat, M. (2010). Prototypes of race and gender: The invisibility of Black women. *Journal of Experimental Social Psychology.*

Shelton, J. N. et al. (2005). Ironic Effects of Racial Bias During Interracial Interactions. *Psychological Science, 16*(5), 397-402.

Sidanius, J. and Pratto, F. (1993). The Inevitability of Oppression and the Dynamics of Social Dominance. In P. Sniderman & P. Tetlock (Eds.), *Prejudice, Politics, and the American Dilemma.* Stanford University Press, pp. 173-211.

Smith, J. M. (1891) *Sketch of the Life and Labors of Rev. Henry Highland Garnet.* Springfield, MA.

Sogyal, R. (1994). *The Tibetan Book of Living and Dying.* New York: HarperCollins.

Spencer, S. J. et al. (1998). Automatic Activation of Stereotypes: The Role of Self-Image Threat. *Personality and Social Psychology Bulletin,* 24, 1139-1152.

Steele, C. (1997). A threat in the air: How stereotypes shape intellectual identity and performance. *American Psychologist, 52*(6), 613-629.

Steele, C. (1999). Thin Ice:" Stereotype Threat" and Black College Students. *The Atlantic Monthly, 284*(2), 44-53.

Stephens et al. (2009). Why did they "choose" to stay? Perspectives of Hurricane Katrina observers and survivors. *Psychological Science.*

Stephenson, J. Z. (2018). "'Real' wages? Contractors, workers, and pay in London building trades, 1650–1800." *Economic History Review*, vol. 71 (1),106-132.

Stepto, G.B. (2003). *The African-American years: Chronologies of American history and experience.* New York: Charles Scribner's Sons/Gale.

Strulik, H., and Weisdorf, J. (2008). "Population, food, and knowledge: a simple unified growth theory." *Journal of Economic Growth* 13.3, 195.

Sue, D.W. (2010). *Microaggressions in everyday life: Race, gender, and sexual orientation.* Hoboken, NJ: Wiley.

Sue, D. W. (2015). *Race Talk and the Conspiracy of Silence: Understanding and Facilitating Difficult Dialogues on Race.*

"Syphilis Study Went On After Its Apparent Success." New York Times, September 13, 1972. Accessed October 5, 2014. http://hn.bigchalk.com/hnweb/hn/do/document?set=search era&&rendition=x-abstract&inmylist=false&urn=urn:proquest:US;PQDOC;H NP;PQD;HNP;PROD;x-abstract;82228133&mylisturn=urn:proquest:US;PQDOC; HNP;PQD;HNP;PROD;x-article-image;82228133&returnpage=.

Tanner, J. (1981). *A history of the study of human growth.* Cambridge University Press.

Tanner, J. (1987). "Growth as a mirror of the condition of society: secular trends and class distinctions." *Pediatrics International,* 29: 96-103.

Thomas, E. (2020). Why do protests turn violent? It's not just because people are desperate. <https://theconversation.com/why-do-protests-turn-violent-its-not-just-because-people-are-desperate-139968

"Tuskegee Syphilis Study Administrative Records, 1929 - 1972." Tuskegee Syphilis Study Administrative Records, 1929 - 1972. Accessed October 5, 2014. http://research.archives.gov/description/281640.

Unzueta, M. M. and B.S. Lowery. (2008). Defining racism safely: The role of self-image maintenance on white Americans' conceptions of racism. *Journal of Experimental Social Psychology, 44*(6), 1491-1497.

Unzueta, M. M. et al. (2008). How believing in affirmative action quotas protects White men's self-esteem. *Organizational Behavior and Human Decision Processes, 105*(1), 1-13.

Van Dyck, T. (1993). *Elite Discourse and Racism.* Newbury Park, CA: Sage Publishers.

Van Sertima, I. (1978). *The African Presence: They Came Before Columbus.* New York: Random House.

Vera, H. and M.G. Andrew (2003). *Screen Saviors: Hollywood Fictions of Whiteness.* Lanham, MD: Rowman & Littlefield Publishers.

Walton and Spencer. (2009). Latent ability: Grades and test scores systematically underestimate the intellectual ability of negatively stereotyped students. *Psychological Science*, 20, 1132-9.

Williams C. (1992). *Destruction of Black Civilization: Great Issues of a Race from 4500 B.C. to 2000 A.D.* Chicago: Third World Press.

Wolfe, C. and Spencer, S. (1996). Stereotypes and prejudice Their overt and subtle influence in the classroom. *American Behavioral Scientist, 40*(2), 176-185.

Wooten, J. T. "Survivor of '32 Syphilis Study Recalls a Diagnosis. "The New York Times, July 27, 1972. Accessed October 7, 2014. http://hn.bigchalk.com/hnweb/hn/do/document?set=search era&&rendition=x-abstract&inmylist=false&urn=urn:proquest:US;PQDOC;H NP;PQD;HNP;PROD;x-abstract;80798514&mylisturn=urn:proquest:US;PQDOC; HNP;PQD;HNP;PROD;x-article-image;80798514&returnpage=.

Word, C. O. et al. (1974). The nonverbal mediation of self-fulfilling prophecies in interracial interaction. *Journal of Experimental Social Psychology, 10*(2), 109-120.

Wray, M. (2006). *Not Quite White: White Trash and the Boundaries of Whiteness*. Durham, NC: Duke University Press.

Williamson, J. (1965). "Regional Inequality and the Process of National Development: A Description of the Patterns." *Economic Development and Cultural Change* 13, 1-84.

WHO. (2013). Review of Social Determinants and the Health Divide in the WHO European Region, World Health Organization, Regional Office for Europe, Copenhagen.

Wilson, A. (1982). Ma Rainey's Black Bottom: A Play. New York, NY: Theatre Communications Group Inc.

Wilson, A. (1992). Two Trains Running: A Play. New York, NY: Samuel French, Inc.

Wu, F. H. (2002). *Yellow: Race in America Beyond Black and White*. New York, NY: Basic Books.

Yates, J. (Culadasa). (2015). *The Mind Illuminated: a complete meditation guide integrating Buddhist wisdom and brain science*. Pearce, AZ: Dharma Treasure Press.

Zuberi, T. and Bonilla-Silva, E. (Eds). (2008). *White Logic, White Methods: Racism and Methodology*. Lanham, MD: Rowman & Littlefield.

Notes: